MW01245839

Tales of the Automazombs

Dreams of Eysan

Tales of the Automazombs: Dreams of Eysan

© 2022 Dex Greenbright

All stories contained in this publication are fiction.
Any resemblance to actual persons living, dead, or undead is
purely coincidental. Rights reserved by the individual authors.

Dex Greenbright, Editor, Cover Artist

ISBN: 978-1-0880-3682-2

Tales of the Automazombs
Dreams of Eysan

Short Stories

Comics

Myths

The World of Automazombs

THE EXPEDITION

By Dex Greenbright

Icy wind whipped against the door flap to Calder's tent. Bursts of arctic air infiltrated every tattered seam. Had he the courage, or stupidity, to peer outside, he would have seen only swirls of white. The blizzard that descended on the camp last night showed no signs of letting up.

Calder adjusted the blanket covering his patient. Lord Barra should have known better than to attempt a rescue of the men and supplies lost in that crevasse. He should have listened to reason. Now the leader of their expedition had hypothermia. There was no wood for a fire, not this far north. Barra refused to accept sharing a bed and the body heat that came with it, but if his condition worsened, Calder wasn't about to let his patient, his friend, die.

He was thankful it was only hypothermia. Some of the team were developing symptoms of illness. The incubation time was oddly long, but he wondered if perhaps the extreme cold had somehow staved off the progression for a time. They mostly coughed, and a few had rashes. Hopefully that would be the whole of it. Lord Barra would not want to delay the expedition any further.

Their last night in civilization was the obvious source of this particular trouble. It was the last village they would see for over a month, so Lord

1

Barra let everyone celebrate with an unending supply of drinks at the tavern. They laughed and danced and talked for hours with the locals. The villagers had just returned from various wintering jobs in the south, and had plenty of tales to tell. One feisty old man had gone as far as Ukketia for a non-Guild mining contract. Looking back, that night was a breeding ground for illness. Calder should have stocked up on curatives.

Calder reached for Lord Barra's pack, hoping for some food, or a drink that wasn't melted snow. Instead, he discovered a brass box with a crank handle and a panel with small holes in it.

"What is this then?"

Lord Barra turned, opening one bleary eyelid.

"Bought it from an inventor several months back. He called it a radio. Said only certain elite citizens had them. Try it."

Calder inspected the device. It had a few dials and gauges, but the crank seemed like the most likely way to power it. He turned it a few times. A dim flicker of light illuminated the gauges. He wound the crank harder, until the machine buzzed. He looked to Lord Barra, sure he'd done something wrong.

Just then, something magical happened. The radio produced a faint melody. It was nearly drowned out by static, but Calder was amazed. He experimented with the dials, and managed to make the music louder and clearer.

He kept the radio powered for a long time. It made his friend visibly calmer. Calder started to nod off himself, when the music ended suddenly.

It was replaced by a Teraltian woman's voice.

"Good evening citizens. In today's news, quarantine zones have been set up in several southern cities, following the deaths of twenty working class individuals. Little is yet known about the illness, but authorities insist that it's nothing a good tonic won't cure."

The news continued on to the affairs of several upper noble families, politics, and a poetic tour of the newest and largest floating city, Caelspyr. But it was the first bit of news that had Calder concerned. Quarantine was nothing to brush off. He counted their team lucky that, though touched by illness, they did not encounter this new and deadly disease. Something terrible was happening at the same time that he had left his medical practice in order to join Lord Barra's expedition to the northern reach.

He couldn't allow himself to feel the pull back toward the capital. His friend needed him here. And venturing out into that blizzard would be foolhardy at best. Calder resumed his search for food, and uncovered a bottle of whiskey and some dried strips of meat wrapped in canvas. He offered them first to Lord Barra, then rationed the rest in case the storm continued.

Over the next few days, Lord Barra's condition stabilized. He and Calder spent much of their time listening to that wondrous radio. During the day, the music helped soothe and heal what medicine alone could not. But Calder began to dread the evenings. It was always the same innocuous tone from the newscaster, and the same implication of a dire problem being ignored.

"More cities across the continent report unusual cases of illness. It is not confirmed that these are the same disease."

Of course it was the same. Why would the government make note of it otherwise?

"A completely irresponsible riot in the Shunniran capital left three dead and a dozen in the hospital."

Calder suspected a good number of those hospitalized were not injured, but infected with whatever pandemic was working its way across the continent.

"Emperor Falkoun the Great has decreed that Caelspyr be opened to any citizens of noble standing, as well as respected merchants, and the Inventors Guild."

They were evacuating the land. Had it gotten so bad, so quickly? And still there was no word about what the disease was, or if anyone was researching a cure. Nobles would always in their own world, it seemed, too far removed from everyday danger that they couldn't recognize the signs.

Calder was one of the best doctors in Teraltis, trained by numerous master scholars at universities in all three countries of the continent. He couldn't ignore what was happening. Not any longer. He knew he had to go home.

3

The blizzard ended early the next morning, and the remaining members of the expedition team were now trickling in to check on their leader. He was able to speak coherently, but shivered and had a weakened heartbeat. Calder insisted that his friend remain in bed.

Lord Barra flatly refused this advice. He struggled to put fresh outer garments on so he could check the sledges.

"If we waste all of our supplies laying about here, we will never reach the north pole!"

"And if you exacerbate your condition and *die*, you will also never reach it."

"Are you the one leading this expedition now?"

Calder's mouth pulled to one side.

"We would have turned around the first time disaster struck if I were. There are so few of us left. I worry we won't make reach the pole despite any efforts we make."

Lord Barra grew quiet for a moment. His hands curled around the edge of the cot.

"This isn't about the expedition at all. You think you can make a difference for those suffering from that preposterous disease."

Calder sighed.

"You know I can. There are people out there who need my expertise."

"And what of those here at camp? I need you here."

The question drew a scowl from Calder. That was entirely unfair. Lord Barra had made it abundantly clear he did not share any of the affection Calder felt. And yet he was willing to manipulate those feelings to get what he wanted. But it wasn't untrue either. Lord Barra was an adventurer to the core, reckless. If Calder left, who would tend the next bout of hypothermia? Or frostbite? Or a broken leg?

In the end, it was Calder who relented. He couldn't force Lord Barra to leave, and venturing back on his own might doom his friend and the rest of the team.

4

They continued their trek north the next day.

The weather was bitterly cold, and the blizzard left deep tracts of snow in its wake. With each labored step, Calder envisioned what damage the pandemic was causing, what lives it disrupted, the families affected.

It was then he realized that none of the team knew any of this was happening. They had a right to know, and if they agreed with him about heading back, Lord Barra would have to reconsider. He would wait until everyone was gathered for dinner. That would be around the time of the evening news bulletin.

Just as planned, when the team sat together with their dinner, Calder revealed what the radio had said.

"I'm afraid we've learned some terrible news."

He proceeded to tell of the disease spreading across the continent, and how it was serious enough that the emperor was evacuating key individuals to that flying playground for the elites of society. Calder couldn't meet Lord Barra's eye. The man was quietly fuming. But that was nothing compared to the team's reaction.

The four men and two women remaining of the expedition were on their feet, shouting at one another and Lord Barra. How long had he known? When were they going to be told? Were their families safe? How bad was this disease? Where was this device that this news purportedly came from?

To that last point, Calder ran to fetch the radio. He turned the crank until it lit up. The news had just barely begun.

"Sad news today as an entire portion of New Clifton is being abandoned due to plague fears."

That was enough to spark a new wave of anger and concern. One of the women stormed over to Lord Barra.

"If our doctor knew, so did you. How could you not tell us? My family is in New Clifton! Or they were. Who knows if they've moved since this happened?"

Calder jumped between them.

5

"I understand your concern, but the blizzard prevented us from sharing this news. And Lord Barra's been unwell. You know this."

"But to march us north instead of south?"

The rest of the team joined her in accusations. Why had they kept going at all? What kind of sick, entitled nobleman would play with the lives of his team like this? Lord Barra shouted furious retorts. The argument escalated. Several of the team were soon wielding tools as weapons. Calder tried to calm both sides down. He was pushed into the snow for his trouble.

The enraged mob lunged at Lord Barra. It was as if the team's minds were no longer their own. The scene reminded him of the news of riots. It couldn't be the same disease, could it? It seemed unlikely, but New Clifton was the closest city to the murky swamp that old-timer had been griping about. The pieces of a terrible puzzle were beginning to assemble in his head.

Calder cursed. He scrambled to his feet. He put himself between the mob and Lord Barra, who was punching every team member who came within range. Calder was beaten with a tent pole, and a knife cut through the outer layer of his coat.

Lord Barra looked far worse. He'd taken a few good hits before Calder could intervene. Bruises marred his face. Blood trickled down from his forehead and into his eye. His leg was bleeding. He had taken up a long knife of his own, and waved it in front of him. They had to get out of there, or the team was going to kill them both.

Calder looked to the sledges. Thank the gods they'd brought reindeer instead of dogs. He grabbed his friend by the coat and hauled him, still shouting, away from the fight. He took the knife and cut one of the reindeer loose.

Lord Barra groaned as he tried to hoist himself up onto the reindeer's back. The gash in his leg was staining his pant leg a deep red. Calder helped his friend up and away from the angry mob. A mallet hit Calder in the ribs, sending a wave of throbbing pain through his chest. There were no more worries about the citizens of Teraltis who could be saved. In the moment, there was only one thought: survive.

He leapt onto the reindeer. The animal jerked at the sudden burden, and of the mob surrounding it. Calder kicked it into a run. It swung its antlers at the mob before bolting.

The camp, the supplies, and their murderous team shrank away to nothing on the horizon. Calder turned to see his friend glaring at him. It was a look of accusation, a look that said 'is this what you wanted?', and ultimately, of defeat. For good or ill, they were going home.

An Impossible Task

By Dex Greenbright

The workshop was awash with blue light as Evellyn sent another pulse of electricity through the probe. The corpse's right arm lifted. She adjusted the probe and tried again. This time, the metal hand grafted to flesh and bone curled into a fist. Evellyn exhaled, relieved; this one movement had taken all week to perfect.

She replaced the probe with delicate copper wires, and sat back to inspect her work thus far. The right arm was now completely mapped out. Those wires were colored red. The legs were tricky, and she was only partially satisfied with their placement. They tended to run at random, which caused damage to the gears in their augmentations. Those wires she marked with blue and green.

The face, left arm, and core muscles would come next. And, of course, the most difficult task still awaited her: connecting the various movements to the metal cap that would control the Automazomb's overall behavior. Would it walk on its own? Could it seek out the plague? Would it devour diseased flesh so the chemicals in its gut could cleanse it? So few of these questions could be answered in the workshop.

Her original design, functional metal legs for those who had been injured, had been a much-needed breakthrough. Combined with the chemists' new method for keeping deceased bodies sturdy, the Automazomb project finally had real potential. The head engineer on the floating city of Kibou had eagerly brought her ideas to the Inventors Guild board. They made copies of her designs and sent them to members across the continent. The namesake of the project and lead financier himself, Lord Thelonious Zomberat, came to her workshop to congratulate her.

Evellyn remembered being so happy about it at first. But the longer she worked on her own experiments, using the grafting technology on the dead instead of the living, the more obstacles she discovered. Her first attempts had overexcited the brain. It became as malleable as living tissue, and had somehow remapped itself, making the Automazomb's movements disjointed. The gods only knew what disaster a less attentive engineer would create. Being so young had its disadvantages; the more advanced Guild members would gladly use her ideas, but rarely heeded her warnings.

Her thoughts were suddenly interrupted by the doors bursting open.

A wide man with slick black hair strode in with a smirk on his face.

"Dear little Evellyn! Hard at work as ever, I see."

Evellyn pushed her goggles up. The historian-turned-inventor walking her way was the first to receive the replacement leg she had designed. He carried a cane, even though in the months since his surgery he had perfected walking on the metal limb. The cane was a symbol of power for him, a token from his noble patron, and he never went anywhere without it. She often wished that of the two historians she knew, that it might have been her friend Liridon who chose to stay on Kibou, and this oaf the one to wander the world.

"Matthias. Will you ever learn to knock?"

"An inventor goes where he pleases. How fares our grisly friend here?"

She pursed her lips. She couldn't help but think that a real inventor would have the sense to knock out of respect for dangerous experiments, if not the Guild member performing them.

The man's smirk faded.

"I don't see much progress on that brain. People are dying. You have the power to save them, yet you delay the launch."

Evellyn glared down at him. He knew precisely which buttons to press.

"You don't think I know that? My parents both gave their lives in studying a cure!" She steadied her breath and unclenched her fists. "It's delicate work. There are a dozen others attempting the same. Have you heard from them? No. Either they've had no luck, or they're being as cautious as I am. So stop pestering me."

Matthias was starting to turn red. Evellyn imagined he hated being told off by someone half his age even more than he hated being denied what he wanted.

He stood in front of her Automazomb, finger raised as if he was going to scold her. But he must have thought better of it, because he turned around and stomped back the way he came.

He paused at the door.

"All of Eysan is relying on you, girl. Get the job done."

Then he was gone.

Evellyn wiped her forehead with her arm. She bit back her frustrated tears; crying wouldn't save anyone. Liridon would have understood her concerns. His love of knowledge was as big as hers for machines. Still, as little as she cared for Matthias, he was right. The plague was killing so many. Whole cities were being abandoned. Her parents had done everything they could to put the world back together. She wasn't about to let them down.

She adjusted the voltage on the probe, and scanned over the remaining movements needing control wires.

"Now, where was I?"

***

Matthias continued to pester her day in and day out.

11

Two weeks went by, and Evellyn barely had an hour to work before that pompous idiot interrupted. Locking the doors did nothing, since inventors were given master keys to every workshop. She managed to complete the arms and legs, and even made the mouth open and close. Next were the eyes. Since they had to determine friend from prey, she knew she had to take drastic measures for privacy.

A mechanic friend gifted her an old lock from the Undercity. There was no way Matthias had a key for this thing. She would be the only one with a key. She spent the early hours removing the standard lock with the replacement.

Evellyn surveyed her handiwork with satisfaction.

"I'd like to see you get through that!"

After securing her workshop, Evellyn had easily the most productive day in working memory. The eyes and arms worked together flawlessly to pick up a ball while avoiding touching the woodpile she'd placed the object in.

She barely noticed the door rattling, or the muffled shouts in the hall.

The next day, Evellyn came in to find a large hole in the doors where the lock had been. She would have laughed if she hadn't been so angry. This was the day she was going to tie all the disparate parts together. If any day needed silence, it was this one.

As if on cue, Matthias strolled into the workshop.

Evellyn gripped the electric probe tight in her hand.

"Can't you give me just one day of…"

Gerald walked in behind her tormentor and task-master. The head engineer on Caelspyr had always been like an uncle to her, and her mentor after her parents died. He didn't look happy.

"Greetings, my dear. Sorry to intrude like this."

"What's going on? Are you alright?"

"I've been brought in to survey your progress. We're running out of time."

12

Evellyn nearly dropped the probe.

"What do you mean?"

"The plague has been spotted on Caelspyr. Quarantines have been set up, but the Guild fears this is only the beginning."

Caelspyr was the biggest, most secure floating city in the world. If the plague struck there, who could be counted safe?

She shook her head.

"It's not ready, sir. It could be months…"

Matthias crossed his arms.

"You have three days."

"What?!"

Evellyn stared at Matthias, completely refusing to believe it could be true. This deadline had to be a cruel, poorly-timed joke.

Matthias's expression was stony, unreadable.

" Lord Zomberat will pull funding by the week's end if no results are produced. And as if you needed further motivation, The Teraltian royal family is personally holding the Guild to the deadline. "

The look of frustration and worry form Gerald stopped Evellyn from arguing further. If her mentor couldn't stall the launch, nobody could.

Satisfied with her silence, Matthias left her and Gerald alone.

Evellyn handed over a spare pair of goggles.

"Hopefully the two of us together can make this work."

***

The pair worked through the night and into the next day, pausing only to eat or fetch another pot of coffee.

It was impossible work; every connection seemed to unmake the previous ones. She was afraid she was doomed to repeat her original failure. But they kept at it, testing and retesting the placement of wires and how they could be applied together.

By the third day, half of the body was fully autonomous. It wasn't enough. Evellyn stormed away from the Automazomb.

Gerald looked up, concerned brows furrowed.

"Where are you off to?"

"They can't be allowed to take him. Not yet."

"We don't have a choice, Evellyn."

Evellyn smirked as she grabbed a welding torch.

"Don't we?"

She added heavy hooks to the door handles and frame, then placed several spare rods across the double doors. She tested the barrier. The doors didn't budge. Her grin remained as she returned to the workbench.

"What's the worst that will happen if I delay us by a few days?"

"We'll both be expelled from the Guild, and forbidden from scientific ventures. Also fined. Possibly jailed. Not to mention the plague could reach this city, kill the aethericists and mechanics who keep Kibou in the skies, and send the whole city crashing down."

Evellyn bit her lip. That was far worse than she imagined. But he hadn't stopped her from barring the doors. He must know as much as she did that it was necessary.

"If they take the Automazomb now and it fails, the consequences will be far worse."

"So, let's quit talking about it and create the impossible."

With one half complete, the second half came much easier. Evellyn was grateful for the help and expertise of her mentor. Perhaps if she hadn't been so stubborn about working alone, she might have been done long ago. But there were so few she worked well with. Some resented her achieving so much while still in her teens, others simply had too different of methods.

Not long after they resumed working, there was a loud thud against the doors.

Matthias peered through the hole where the lock had been. His cheeks were flushed beet red.

"What do you think you're doing? Open this door immediately!"

Evellyn turned to Gerald.

"I didn't think to cover the hole."

"Nothing to be done about it now. Take this wire here?"

She held the red-painted wire while Gerald soldered the connection to the control cap. They were nearly done now, against all the odds.

Imperial guards were summoned. They called for Gerald and Evellyn to release the project before it was too late. Evellyn's hand shook. What if the punishments ahead of them were even worse than Gerald thought? What if they were killed? They were so close to finishing now.

Gerald placed his hand over hers.

"Nearly there, child. Just a few more connections now."

She nodded. The voices from the hall pounded against her ears, but she couldn't let them get to her. She couldn't make a mistake now. Not in these last critical moments.

The two carefully soldered the last of the wires. The cap was finally complete. They lowered it over the open portion of the Automazomb's skull. They sewed the skin back in place, as much as it could be. Gerald secured the edges of each metal plate with small rivets.

Evellyn carefully surveyed the completed Automazomb. It looked perfect, or as much as a metal-grafted, plague-eating corpse contraption possibly could. Still, there was a nagging fear at the back of her mind. Why had no other engineers succeeded?

She sighed.

"We need to test it before we unbar the door. I would take another week if we could. It would be stupid to call it complete before we're sure everything went how we expected."

Gerald didn't respond.

Evellyn looked over. Her mentor was staring at the doors. The guards, the inventors, Matthias, they were all gone.

"Did they give up?"

Gerald gave her a worrying look.

"Cooped up in my lab, I was the last to hear when--"

Just then, a siren blared. Then another, closer to the building. Evellyn thought she heard shouting in the streets.

Gerald flew into a panic. He raced to the doors and pulled the barrier free.

"It's exactly the same as Caelspyr. I knew it was only a matter of time. The plague has come!"

"But you said they dealt with the plague there. The city isn't crashing. The authorities will put up a quarantine and all will go back to normal in a day or two."

"And what if this is the area infected? The Guild needs us. Every member should be heading toward the nearest airship. Where do *you* think Matthias went?"

Evellyn hurried after her mentor, who was running down the abandoned hallway.

"You're sure? But the Automazomb! My notes! They're all scattered. We have to--"

"No time! We need to escape before we are trapped here."

16

When they got outside, they were swept up in the crowd. A voice called out instructions through a speaking trumpet. Everyone was talking, everyone was scared, but that commanding voice echoed through the streets, guiding them.

"This is an evacuation. All citizens of the northern quarter, head to the warehouse airship docks."

Evellyn kept close to Gerald. It wasn't until they reached the docks that the truth was revealed. A woman in an official uniform held the speaking trumpet everyone had been following. She was smiling. She stood on a platform at the entrance to the docks.

"A hearty thanks to the Inventors Guild for organizing this first plague drill in Kibou's northern quarter. Such drills will be conducted periodically to ensure our safety."

The crowd was livid about the scare. They shouted insults as the official insisted that true preparation meant the drills had to be unscheduled.

Evellyn knew better. The timing was too perfect. She grabbed Gerald's sleeve.

"Matthias made this happen. We have to get back!"

The two raced back to the Guild complex. Evellyn pushed a pair of aethericists aside, desperate to reach her workshop before Matthias or anyone else got there. Without additional tests for safety and accuracy, what good was any of it?

Up ahead, she could see the doors to her workshop thrust wide. Had she left them that way? Please, anyone, say that she had!

Evellyn's heart dropped as she reached the doorway.

It was all gone.

The Automazomb. Her notes - even the ones that had nothing to do with this project. All of it.

Even as tears filled her eyes, she strengthened her resolve. The others had to be warned. Gerald would help her. Even if they wouldn't listen to her, they had to listen to him. He was a head engineer!

By that evening, they were given an audience with the Guild heads of Kibou. It was determined that nothing could be done. There was no evidence that the Automazomb had been stolen. The head inventor went so far as to claim it must have walked away on its own, taking her notes with it. Everyone laughed while Evellyn quietly fumed.

Frustrated and humiliated, Evellyn and Gerald were forced to give up. She was assigned to a different project, and he was sent home to Caelspyr in disgrace.

Within a week, word came in from all over Eysan. Guild members everywhere had stumbled upon the breakthrough that allowed for the completion of the first wave of Automazombs. A test launch would begin in the old capital shortly. Gerald confirmed what Evellyn suspected: her notes had been copied and sent to every corner of the continent.

To make matters worse, while Evellyn was given minor credit, Matthias was listed as the project's lead. Lord Zomberat held a ceremony, praising the Guild for completing this work months ahead of the proposed deadline. Matthias was to be given an advanced rank within the inventors for making this acceleration possible.

Evellyn knew then that she had been used. All she could do was hope the other engineers would have the resolve to insist on further testing before any Automazombs set foot on the ground.

GOING HOME

By Dex Greenbright

A string of villages hugged the southern rim of Beskra canyon. In the time before the plague, they mined the canyon walls for minerals. A train arrived each season to sell the material abroad.

Their isolation kept the great plague at bay. The devastation of the first waves of death were felt in a different way. The trains no longer shuttled away goods from the canyon. There was no one to need such things, or pay for them. Instead, the trains brought refugees from Teraltis and from the same Shunniran cities the villagers once relied on for their livelihoods. Beskra was quickly becoming the most populous land in all of Eysan.

As careful as these strangers thought they were, the plague followed them. The last safe place in the world had been soiled. Masks once used to keep out mining dust now served as a weak barrier against certain death. The vast canyon that had given them life became a mass grave. Any who carried the plague were thrown in with the dead, all in the name of protecting uninfected families.

But without the mines, there was not enough money to bring in the supplies they needed. Medicine, food, even fresh water was scarce. One by one, the villages were abandoned for the larger town of Ferro that rested below the Grand Library of Ontaakh.

The flyers had been posted all over Ferro. The canyonlands were to be cleaned by Automazombs – metal men who could destroy the plague. Satoru saw it as a sign they could finally go home. It was nearly half of his life ago when they'd fled. More than anything he wished to make things go back to the way they were, when he could chase hares and climb the canyon wall. His parents refused his pleas to take the family home.

Armed only with a rucksack filled with bread and his father's canteen, Satoru had set out to prove them wrong. It wasn't dangerous anymore. Once he'd gotten proof that the plague had been cleaned from Beskra, he would bring them all back. All of the villagers and even the strangers who'd brought the plague. Everyone could go home and life would be normal again.

Satoru walked to the canyon's edge and sat with his legs dangling over the cliff. The spyglass Master Scholar Bernard had given him was finally more than a toy to make his sister look far away. Now it would make the little figures at the bottom of the canyon bigger than ants. He held the device up to his eye and adjusted the little crank that moved the glass pieces.

He gasped as the metal men came into focus. He fell back. His heart pounded. The metal men were monsters! They had metal parts, sure, but... they were made from corpses. Their eyes glowed like fire. Sickening brown smoke billowed out of pipes on their backs. Their hands dug in like claws, grabbing the dead off the ground and pulling them up toward gnashing mouths full of teeth and grinding gears.

Satoru crawled back to the edge. He stuck only the spyglass over into the chasm this time. As terrifying as it was, he had to look. This was somehow going to be the way the world was saved. He couldn't turn away.

There were a dozen, maybe even twenty of the metal monsters eating, clanging, and lumbering at the bottom of the canyon. Even more were streaming in. Some had wheels where legs used to be. Others were missing limbs and had them replaced with weapons that hacked into their dead victims. Chunks of diseased flesh flew everywhere. The bits that fell were picked up by the next wave of metal men and eaten like the rest.

He recognized the body of the blacksmith from his village. Satoru covered his mouth to stop from crying out as the man's face was torn off. Satoru didn't want to think of what the monsters might do if they found him. They ate like wild beasts. Down in the canyon, flesh was ripped from bone. The machine men roared in their metal voices. Not a single body was left untouched.

As he adjusted his position for a better view, his elbow slipped. A few loose stones tumbled over the edge. The commotion drew the attention of a monster below. Satoru spotted the thing's glowing eyes staring back at him - through him. He scrambled to his feet and ran. He didn't care what the Inventors' flyer said. Home would never be safe again.

← mental stimulation
  (electric)

← imaging/food sensor

← jaw augmentation

22

Not Safe For Work

By Victoria Bitters

Madame Wyniera,

I hope this letter finds you well.

When last we met, you expressed interest in the Automazombs and vexation at your difficulties in studying them "up close". I had assumed that those difficulties arose from the machines sensing dead flesh outside of their designated zones. But! I recently encountered one that attacked dead and living alike - right in front of me, no less.

A friend (and highly skilled engineer) studied this malfunctioning device and determined that all the programmatic wiring and structures were operating as intended. The only notable difference between this machine and a recently-deployed Automazomb appears to be the slurry that operates as the mechanical's 'digestive humors', meant to ingeniously destroy the plague.

I remembered your mention of a comrade — or was he a servitor? — known as "Doctor Grumpy" who possesses the skills of a chemist. I hope the two of you are still acquainted, because I would like to set the both of you to the task of uncovering the cause of an Automazomb's erratic behavior. I've taken the liberty to discreetly have the Automazomb in question delivered with this message. Experiment with it as necessary, but do take care of it. The fate of our world may rest on your discovery.

Eagerly awaiting your findings,

Jaff wheeled a large crate into the lab. The large man, generally imperturbable, was flushed from the effort, pale hairs clinging to his broad forehead. As the servant eased the container down with a grunt, something within shifted, knocking against the side of the box with a loud *thunk*.

Dietrich eyed the box sidelong. He wasn't aware of any particular equipment that was supposed to be delivered, but then, his 'noble employer' – or mad quasi-benefactor, to be more accurate – rarely kept him abreast of her schemes. At least until she needed him to replace some mechanism she'd destroyed, or to devise a way to accomplish her latest bat-brained 'experiment'. Or if she was bored. Gods all help them if she was bored.

The lad, Djermay, who was ostensibly Dietrich's to command since his late master's ...departure, sidled away from the box. The boy preferred the bench furthest from the door, but that put him next to the wide open space aport, where Jaff had deposited the box. Djermay moved starboard, to the second-to-last of four benches that lined the fore wall of the laboratory. Three more lined the aft wall, bracketing the door, with another three benches in the center of the room, each overhung with tools and vessels and littered with debris – components and chemicals, notes and prototypes.

Jaff ignored the occupants of the room and scanned the benches for a clear spot to leave a battered envelope with his employer's name scrawled on the outside: *Lady Wyniera Mudassme*. This being a fruitless task, he eventually assumed a parade rest several steps from the door, envelope in hand, waiting for her to arrive.

Dietrich checked a chronometer – it was nearly midday. There was some sort of breakfast the young noble had to attend in order to wring funding out of her family. She'd complained about it for hours the prior evening, occasionally threatening to drag him along with her. It was hard to tell if she was in earnest or just tormenting him to cheer herself up. His personal motto, developed specifically for dealing with Lady Wyn but applicable to most other aspects of his life was: Always assume the worst. Nevertheless, he'd been left unmolested this morning and Dietrich didn't imagine she would return for several more hours.

But Jaff must have had better information – he usually did – and it was only a quarter hour before the young woman burst into the room with her characteristic exuberance and complete disregard for delicate equipment.

24

The doors bounced off the wall and the nearest bench, rattling tools and cabinetry. Happily, nothing broke, this time.

"Where is it? What is it?" Lady Wyn snatched the envelope out of her servant's hand and ripped it open eagerly.

"How can you be this worked up about you-don't-even-know-what?" Dietrich demanded, foolishly trying to apply logic to the situation. He just couldn't seem to stop himself.

"I know that that historian I've run into a time or two, always in the most entertaining circumstances, sent me something. The man is a complete disaster-magnet. It will be marvelous."

Apprehension and anxiety unfurled in Dietrich's gut. The apprehension was easily explained – anything that made Lady Wyn happy was probably going to be horrifying. And any time she spoke admiringly of another's skills, Dietrich worried that his own precarious harbor was in jeopardy.

The young woman gasped in obvious delight. Manically waving the paper at Dietrich, she very nearly pranced in place.

"It's a machine!"

"That does...?"

"It eats people!"

Dietrich and Jaff both stared at her, at the box, then back at Lady Wyn. The stoic servant was definitely having an expression, now.

"That... doesn't sound like a... *good* machine," Dietrich eventually said.

"No, no – ah, I'm saying it wrong, I'm so- It eats *dead* people. Except this one has been eating living people, too. This is all very exciting!"

Dietrich finally realized that she was referring to the machines that were performing 'clean up' for the amazingly virulent plague, the Automazombs. Except that made it worse.

"You mean to say that a disease-immersed, mechanical carrion beast – that is misfiring so badly as to murder people – has been delivered. To you." Looking about the room for someone to exchange horrified glances with, Dietrich noticed the boy was missing again. Djermay somehow managed to disappear whenever Lady Wyn showed up. Dietrich mentally applauded the lad's excellent survival instincts, but was still annoyed at the lack of solidarity. Jaff was typically useless for commiseration, and had indeed quickly recovered from the shock, reverting to his usual blank demeanor.

"Would it save some time if I just set the city on fire and threw myself into a meat grinder now...?"

Lady Wyn gave him one of her 'how droll you are' looks, shoved the letter into his hand, and hauled Jaff over to the box to begin unpacking her monstrosity.

Reading the note, Dietrich vacillated between appalled and annoyed. It was theoretically flattering that this man thought that Dietrich could discover the source of the malfunction. It was actually unnerving that anyone would think that involving Lady Wyn in any kind of life-and-death problem-solving would improve matters. Yes, he was pleased that Lady Wyn had mentioned him and his skills, particularly if she had called him a colleague. No, he didn't like the nickname she kept bandying about, but it's not as if he'd be happier if she was telling people his real name.

The mention of discolored chemicals nagged at him. That indicated that a contaminant had made it into what was already a volatile mixture, from what he recalled of the machines' development. Dietrich was already envisioning the chemical tests he would need to run to discover the composition of the solution when the loud *crack!* of the box being opened startled him from his revery.

The slumped shape within the box seemed human enough, at first. Wispy strands of dark hair stuck out from a depleted scalp. Scraps of linen were wrapped around the arms and legs, dangling down and disguising the modifications that had been made to the man's corpse. When Dietrich managed to nerve himself enough to approach, he saw the metal sticking out from the joints. Taut skin that gave the figure an appearance of youth, from a distance, proved to be ashen and verging on shredding where it was affixed to the mechanical joints that allowed the deceased to be animated. Instead of eyes, flat red-tinted lenses occupied hollow sockets. Bulging lips and cheeks hinted at the replacement teeth that lurked within the re-made man's slack mouth. Closer-to, Dietrich could see the mechanisms sticking up from the body, at the back of the skull and along the spine, as well as the dangling loops of tubing, draped over the corpse's shoulder and sagging

26

from its stomach, coated with a dark, oily-looking substance. The smell emanating from the box was acrid and musty.

Flourishing a pair of insulated gauntlets, Lady Wyn impatiently gestured for Jaff to help her remove the machine from its packing. The large man – gloveless, himself – stiffly gripped one arm, where the linen cloth offered some barrier. When Lady Wyn pulled, the figure lurched out of the box. With a hissed breath, Jaff jerked himself out of the way, letting the creature collapse most of the way to the floor. Dietrich didn't even try to suppress his own recoil. He'd never played a role in any of the direct mechanisms for the Automazomb project, during his time with the Guild. There had never been a need to get comfortable with corpses.

Lady Wyn tched her annoyance with the skittish men and yanked on the machine, to no effect. She was strong for her size and gender, but the body was heavy with augmentations. Filled with perfectly justified unease, Dietrich dragged over one of the metal stands that served as forms when shielding plates needed to be hammered out. He and Lady Wyn wedged it under the Automazomb while Jaff worked to heave the body up onto the prop in small bursts, his face wrinkled faintly with distaste.

They were all panting when a sharp knock sounded at the door. Dietrich hurriedly grabbed a drop cloth and flung it over the body. Then he asked himself why exactly he had done that.

Lady Wyn rolled her eyes at him and strode toward the door.

"That will be the engineer the historian sent along, to give us background on the mechanisms."

Lady Wyn flung open the door, revealing a woman, her dark hair tied back with a what looked like a net of green ribbons. She seemed startled by Lady Wyn, jerking back slightly, but the reactions of others never gave the noblewoman pause. She seized the woman by both forearms and towed her into the room.

"Excellent timing. We've just decanted the device. Show us how it works!"

The woman's copper-flecked eyes widened and she got the expression that the unaccustomed tended to settle upon when meeting Lady Wyn for the first time – halfway between astonished and aghast, thoroughly shot through with uncertainty. Given the Lady's forthright confidence, people often came to the conclusion that any misunderstanding must be their own error.

"Didn't you...? The problem is that it doesn't work. I thought Liridon sent a letter to explain the situation?"

The engineer – Dietrich could now see she wore the emblem of that Guild, however discreetly, as well as the telltale stains and calluses of one who worked with machines barehanded – indicated the poorly cloaked Automazomb, as if to ensure they were speaking of the same object.

"Yes, yes, not as intended, but things that break from expectations are more *interesting*. No? Well, to each their own, or so I'm told. Show us how it's supposed to work, then."

Giving herself a small shake, the engineer turned her attention to the machine. She pulled the cloth off and gestured at the exposed mechanical spine and a plate that served at the cover to the back of the skull. What followed was a technical stream of pneumatics and end effectors and rotational frequencies and wiring schema and resistance and – Dietrich could follow, but he didn't particularly want to, not when phrases like "substitute for ruptured ligament", "repurposed intestinal sheathe", and "bone screws" kept cropping up.

After a lengthy explanation, with increasingly disturbing cross-examination from Lady Wyn, the engineer confessed herself parched. Lady Wyn was impatient to continue, but she had (eventually) developed an understanding that the bare minimum maintenance of others' human needs was required to get the results she wanted. Dietrich took some pride in his role in helping to lower the Lady's expectations of how many privations people could endure and still be "useful".

Lady Wyn released the engineer – still unnamed, which was probably for the best. Introductions tended to be a two-way experience and Dietrich preferred his anonymity, especially with Guild members. Jaff led her away to be fed, watered, and adequately rested, so that the Lady's interrogation could resume. Dietrich briefly assumed that meant that he could rest as well, before being disabused of this notion when the Lady hefted a spanner with entirely too much enthusiasm.

'What are you doing?' was never a question that Dietrich had enjoyed having answered by Lady Wyn. Deciding that discretion was the better part of valor, he moved his tools to the farthest work station and left her to her no doubt ill-advised meddling.

Unsettling squelches, metallic rattles and hisses, and meaty *thunks* filled the air. Dietrich poured all his concentration into setting up the assays he would run on the chemical and biological samples.

He didn't know the exact composition of the reductive mixture that should be present, but he was relatively sure that vitrolic acid and copper were in the mix. A solution of horseradish root, coal tar, and zia-novallin (known to the lay chemist as 'essense of firefly') should give him some data to work with. The final component needed for the assay would be bile acid. As unpleasant as that was to obtain, the alternate ingredient for preparing this standard mixture was condensed vitrolic air. Having first-hand experience of the tragic volatility of vitrolic air, Dietrich would rather deal with 'disgusting' than 'eagerly explosive'.

He had reached the point where he was ready to start adding samples when Dietrich realized that the perturbing noises had died down. Glancing over his shoulder, he saw Lady Wyn scowling at the slumped machine. She had reattached various tubes and wires and resealed the skull plate over the mass of copper wires and electranum spikes that protruded from the sunken brain that was the substrate for the mechanism's unnerving control system. Dietrich supposed that it made sense that the Lady would try to see if she could put the machine back together. He was just more used to seeing her take things apart, usually to their detriment. In this situation, surely *less mess* was the better option. That didn't stop him from feeling decidedly uneasy at seeing the Automazomb theoretically 'ready to go'.

Clearing his throat, Dietrich gestured with a syringe at the device that was failing to live up to the Lady's expectations. In his right hand, he held a 'honeycomb' – a many-sectioned dish perfect for clustering assorted samples – ready to fill. Lady Wyn muttered indistinctly about delays and waved him onward as she stalked out of the laboratory, slamming the door behind her.

Dietrich was breathing shallowly as he tweezed a mostly-liquid gob of matter from the corner of the Automazomb's mouth when he heard a gasp and clattering behind him. Jumping back and only just avoiding dropping the honeycomb, he spun to see Djermay, stuttering and pointing at the machine with obvious horror.

29

"Q'ua's pen, lad!" Dietrich huffed, rattled. He dropped the latest sample into a section of the tray and waved the boy back as he set the container on the nearest bench with shaking hands. "Yes, it's dreadful, dangerous, and the embodiment of a terrible decision-making process, but that's hardly unique in this lab. If you're going to boggle at every monstrosity-"

A low hiss from behind him that rapidly rose to a shrill whistle interrupted Dietrich's irritable rant. Without even looking back – because turning to face a threat was as much of a waste of time as boggling – Dietrich sprinted to the end of the first bench and made sure it was between him and the machine. Djermay dropped out of sight, which was an acceptable initial strategy, but Dietrich couldn't spare the time to track the lad – he had a monstrosity to deal with.

The reconstructed Automazomb's flat red ocular lenses slowly began to glow and the sagging head was the first part to move, disturbingly isolated from the rest of the figure. The skull lifted, angling upward to the point that a living neck would protest, and beyond. The skin around the gullet frayed further, showing the outlines of metallic tubing. It was... looking at him. Dietrich shivered and started groping for a weapon, not willing to take his eyes off the machine. His hand closed on something just as the Automazomb's four limbs all jerked at once. Swearing, he flung his impromptu missile – a hefty rotor armature with a corroded coil – at the mechanism as he darted back another bench-length. He missed the head, unfortunately, but the component struck a shoulder joint, causing the monstrous device to topple off of the shielding that was propping it up.

Dietrich had barely begun to mentally congratulate himself when the Automazomb rolled, landing on forearms and knees. Lurching forward as the lower limbs straightened, the machine smashed its face into the ground, causing Dietrich to wince in inadvertent sympathy.

Which was clearly misplaced, as the Automazomb simply planted its hands and levered itself upright, unconcerned with the flattening of its former nose, which now sagged over the slightly gaping mouth or the bloodlike concoction that oozed from the wound. It rose to its full height, shambling forward and careening off of the benches, but keeping its head pointed at him. Panting with fear, Dietrich scrambled back toward the last bench – which was up against the starboard wall. If he could just keep the wide spanse of sturdy wood and metal between himself and the machine- The Automazomb cut off that scarcely formed hope as it staggered around the second center bench, angling straight for him. This briefly caused it to bounce off of the fore port corner of the workstation, but it corrected itself quickly.

Dietrich snatched up a contraption of the Lady's design, a long tube with a pump on the back end and a bulbous muzzle, a thick reservoir bulging out of the center. Fumbling with the device Lady Wyn gleefully referred to as a spitfire, Dietrich stumbled back, slamming into the fore starboard-most bench. He succeeded in deploying the flint trigger and plunged the pump by jamming it into his own stomach.

With a belch, roiling flames burst from the bulb, drenching the Automazomb in burning fuel. Dietrich yelped and flung himself to the right as the machine, on fire, kept coming. It half sprawled over the bench, its arms grasping wildly and scooping the assorted contents on the surface towards its gaping, gnashing maw. Scrambling backward on hands and feet, Dietrich reached for the next bench's countertop, to pull himself up, when Lady Wyn suddenly appeared, darting toward the machine, her arms and torso canted to one side in an apparent charge.

Within scant feet of the Automazomb, her arms thrust forward and Dietrich glimpsed the crowbar she was wielding like a spear. The tip slammed into the back of the head, angling in and upward, scooping out a hefty chunk of the skull's contents. Char and metal and scorched flesh spattered the wall. The machine spasmed twice, then collapsed.

Gasping for breath led to coughing on the stench of burning meat and chemicals. Dietrich crouched next to the bench and tried to marshal his arguments.

"You... activated it," he rasped, eventually.

Lady Wyn had been thumping her crowbar – slick with gore – against the floor in frustration as she glowered at the device that had thoroughly disappointed her. She sighed and a sulky expression settled over her face.

"Of course. And it took a ridiculously long time to actually get started, didn't it? I've never been able to observe one in a controlled environment."

"Controlled?" Dietrich wheezed, hauling himself upright in indignation. "You are the opposite of control in every way!"

The young noble arched an eyebrow at her agitated inventor. "Really? Because I'm not smacking you with a wrench and you're being quite provoking. Would you like me to stop *controlling* my reactions, then?"

"...No."

Lady Wyn huffed wryly and let the crowbar clatter to the floor. She frowned at the burning Automazomb and waved her hand vaguely in front of her.

"It wasn't very hardy, either. A little fire, a blow to the head... it certainly didn't hold up any better than the living do."

Dietrich couldn't even manage to be appalled. His heart was finally slowing and the weariness he often felt after a discussion with Lady Wyn was sinking in.

"Unreliable, inefficient, inelegant... and so very limited in its capabilities." Lady Wyn humphed over the shortcomings of the device. "*My* automata will be able to do so much more than merely consume the plague's leavings."

Dietrich sagged against the bench. Of course she would want to build a greater monster.

"...You don't mean 'more' as in 'cure the plague'. You mean 'more' as in... I don't know, blow up corpses or some other deeply disturbing idea that you are convinced would be 'scientifically relevant'. Because... you're you."

Lady Wyn blinked at him. "Are you advocating corpse explosions? That doesn't sound like you. You usually seem opposed to all sorts of explosions. Maybe you should go rest."

"That's not what I-" Dietrich sighed. "...Yes. Maybe I should."

"Meanwhile, I'll start studying viable corpse explosion metho-"

"NO."

TALES OF THE AUTOMAZOMBS

The New Crewman

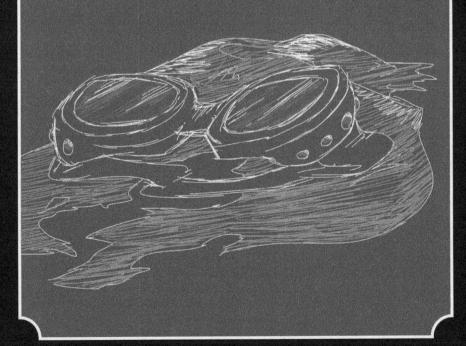

35

36

37

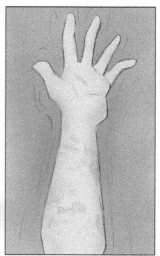

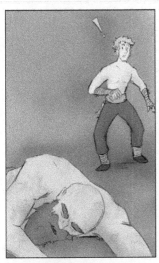
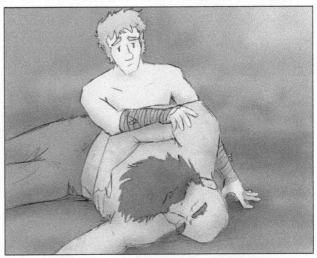

Greetings, friend.

40

TALES OF THE AUTOMAZOMBS

The Letters
of Subira Hawke

My dearest Evellyn,

I hope this letter finds you untouched by plague or other hardship. I am not as dead as the papers suggest. My latest invention did not "burn a great fireball in the sky." Our airship was forced to land by the Shunniran government, and we were sentenced to quarantine in the ports of Djimbuk. We salvaged some of the equipment and supplies. The ship itself was destroyed by the authorities. They fear the plague above all. Did they not realize our mission was to discover the source and find a cure? Now I worry our research will be just as delayed as we are. I must tell you, it is a strange thing, being trapped on the island of my birth. I wanted to share this part of your history with a visit, but not now. And not like this.

Write if you can, but don't come. The Djimbuka have grown suspicious of anyone traveling from the mainland.

All my love,

Subira Hawke

Illustration of a tragedy offshore Djimbuk: Inventors airship crash, killing over sixty.

An airship belonging to the Inventors Guild crashed today, just offshore of the Shunniran island of Djimbuk. Authorities suspect the Guild members were contaminated with plague, causing their experiments to backfire. Noteable Inventor Subira Hawke was among the crew. Clearly, an overzealous pursuit of science has once again endangered the masses. Who among us can say for certain that the Inventors Guild themselves did not conjur up this plague, that they might have a problem requiring their narrow skillset to solve?

Beloved Evellyn,

My shipmates and I - Guild members and crew alike - remain clean of all plague symptoms. We take every precaution. Our corner of the port is separated from the rest of the town by a small inlet used as a marina. When we do venture out, we wear protective clothing and masks. The same kind as your young Scholar friend used when collecting samples for us. This being said, we could not sit idly while so many are suffering. We set up a tent, and have begun offering medical services. Our food is also shared when rations fall short.

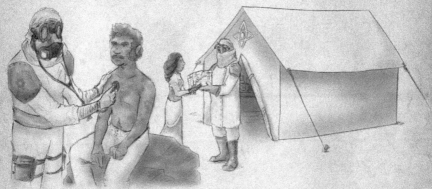

I met a young woman who reminds me of you. She has an adventurer's heart. She routinely takes a small boat and fishes at the deepest border of the quarantine zone, despite the guards threatening to burn the boat and confiscate her catches. If circumstances were different, the two of you might have been fast friends.

Until my next letter, I wish you well.

All my love,

Subira Hawke

My sweet Evellyn,

As a service to the plague victims, my team writes out messages to their families. These are all clean, of course, but I have seen the authorities burning letters! It breaks my heart. I can only pray that my own letters are reaching you, but I have doubts. Despite this, I refuse to give up hope. If even one makes it to you, it will be enough.

Here I am assisting in the creation of our first treatment for the Mad Plague.

More of the quarantine residents have come to us, hoping to help in the search for a cure. Is it possible that our forced landing could be the biggest breakthrough in solving this pandemic? We have now studied the plague in greater bredth and depth than ever before. Using what we've learned, our Chemists think they might be able to make a useful treatment to lessen the worst of the symptoms. I am eager to test it. We must begin somewhere!

All my love,

Subira Hawke

Dearest daughter,

The young woman from my last letter has agreed to allow my team to study her condition. Here is a sketch of her, running tests with us. It is my hope that our observations will become a basis for our research once the quarantine is lifted. We are hopeful this will lead to a cure.

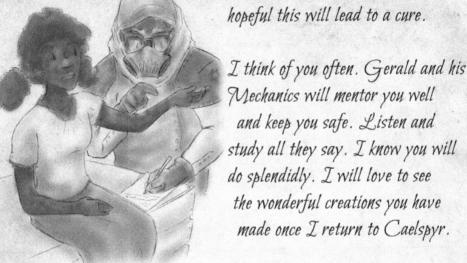

I think of you often. Gerald and his Mechanics will mentor you well and keep you safe. Listen and study all they say. I know you will do splendidly. I will love to see the wonderful creations you have made once I return to Caelspyr.

More people are sentenced to quarantine every day. The crew is worried about overpopulation. The inlet only acts as a buffer if the ill remain on the other side. Some of my team have begun wearing filtration masks around our quarters. But, don't fret. We are still well, and I will come home to you as soon as I am allowed.

The airship captain and crew playing Trickster's Hand

All my love,

Subira Hawke

45

Dear Evellyn,

I must preface today's letter and tell you that I am fine. The worst is over. I wonder, what news has reached you of the riots? Unlike our downed airship, this catastrophy was my fault. I approved the treatments, despite a lack of testing. Pain was lessened by half, but the plague-rage worsened. They fought each other, before crossing the inlet. They destroyed our medical tent, and half our food stores. The airship crew defended my team. Two became infected. Another was killed. The rioters then moved on to the barriers.

It was a terrible sight. The guard houses were overrun. Eventually, the Shunniran army quelled the violence. Any building touched by the rioters was burnt. They also destroyed my team's remaining stores as punishment. They started burning our research too, but I hid our most important notes. I hope you never have to bear the pain of your life's greatest work being destroyed.

All my love,

Subira Hawke

Dear Evellyn,

The riots ruined our camp. Only a third can still be considered clean. Two of my team have contracted the plague. Their spirits are high so far, and they're using it as an opportunity to learn. All of science appreciates their bravery.

It's been a terrible weight, knowing we caused this. But far worse has been the aftermath. The authorities are brutal. Nearly half the plague victims were killed, even those who did not riot. Their bodies were stored in a pier house. Our Chemists think this was a mistake. Several crewmen who ate fish caught near are now ill. It looks like we've found yet another way the Mad Plague spreads.

I have more sad news. The young woman I spoke of has succumbed to the plague. Every new treatment falls short. I miss you, Evellyn. I cannot wait until this ordeal is over and I can be with you again.

All my love,

Subira Hawke

Evellyn,

Every precaution has failed. I write now from the shore at the very edge of the quarantine zone. The plague victims didn't know it was our treatment that set off the riots. Now they do. The camp burns. I can still hear my friends screaming. Only four of us made it out.

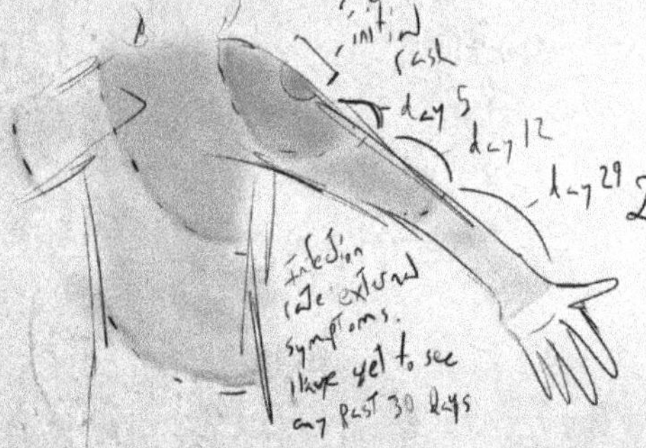

I was wounded during my escape. I know in my heart I am infected. This will be my last letter.

One of the Chemists who escaped with me just handed me something. My letters! None were ever sent, but neither were they destroyed as I feared. I have a renewed chance of reaching you!

I am writing this letter on a page of research notes. The rest of our work will be in with the letters. Take them to the lead Inventor. Use them. Make sure this type of thing never happens again.

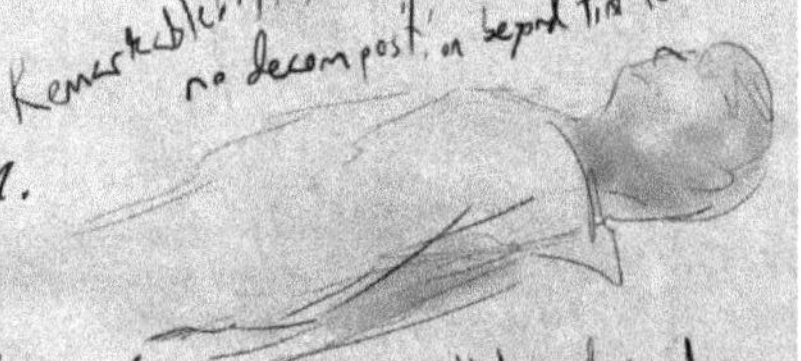

Shifting Yaim'allelo, guide this bottle through your waters. Let it reach my beloved daughter with haste.

All my love,

Subira Hawke

48

The Birth of Ershk-gula

By Dex Greenbright

There is an old story, one recited most often by the priestesses of Eyso in the north, that I wish to tell you now. It is the origin of the Dark Lady Ershk-gula. It is the story of Death.

- *Liridon MaRaukna*

Eyso, Her Magnificent Vastness, was born on the side of order. The land was sturdy and grew plants in a predictable fashion. D'alor was and ever will be an agent of chaos, constantly changing day to night and back again. Many now say that Earth and Sky were made for one another, two parts of a whole, but the gods who created them did not see that at the time. When Eyso and D'alor fell in love, Grandmother and Grandfather fought terribly.

Grandmother Rau-cilla, embodiment of chaos, shouted out great storms that swirled wildly to tear away at Order. Grandfather Q'ua, realization of order, penned mountains and ice to crush Chaos into submission. The other gods could do little but watch. Order and Chaos were the most powerful beings by far, and the others feared they would cease to exist If they intervened. But the fight could never end, for chaos and order are equals.

Only Ahmetz the Just knew he could not sit idly. It was not right that Rau-cilla create gods that would tempt his sister Eyso away. Grandmother abused her powers so as to destroy all that was good and right. This was a simple fact, he thought! Ahmetz saw himself as Grandfather's enforcer, the one made to guide others true. He would be the one to bring a conclusive end to the disorderly.

He walked stealthily around the edge of the battleground, wielding his famed knife. The blade of Justice was coated with his own blood, capable of slaying any beast. He had used it many a time to kill monsters created by the shortsighted gods who sided with chaos. He used it, too, against any people of Eysan who defied rule and order. Now he would use it against Chaos herself. Ahmetz knew the magic within the blade would surely weaken her so that Grandfather might finally prevail.

As Ahmetz waited in the shadows for the perfect time to strike, his sister Eyso saw the glinting of the blade. She realized her brother's plot. She shouted a warning to Rau-cilla, creator of the god she loved. But Grandmother did not hear. The battle was thunderously loud that Eyso's words failed to reach her.

So Eyso used all of her powers of the land to lend her speed as she ran across the battlefield. She had to reach Ahmetz before this most terrible attack could occur. The goddess of the land is steady and grounded; she is a goddess of balance. What her brother thought to be fact was only hatred and jealousy wearing a mask. Chaos and Order were both needed for life to exist.

Q'ua pushed Rau-cilla back with a wall of ice. This was Ahmetz's chance. Justice raised his blood-knife. He lunged forward to attack with keen, singular focus. Unable to warn Rau-cilla of the danger, Eyso jumped into the path of the blade.

The knife struck her gut with tremendous force. Her cry of anguish caused Grandmother and Grandfather to pause their fighting. Ahmetz was horrified. His hand slipped away from the knife.

Eyso fell to the ground. But she did not bleed. The magical blood on the knife of Justice, combined with the souls of all it had killed, melded

50

with the goddess's own life-giving body. When she drew out the knife, a dark hand held firmly to the blade. Eyso pulled harder, and a new goddess was brought into the world. Her skin was tinted purple, and the whites of her eyes were dark as night.

This new goddess was Ershk-gula. She embodied the death that would have been Eyso's, that could have been Rau-cilla's. She took the knife from Eyso, and bowed low out of respect for her mother. Ahmetz staggered back as Death walked toward him with his own knife.

Ershk-gula laughed at her father's fear.

"It is clear that you cannot properly judge when it is death's time. I will keep this knife. It will become *my* symbol and all shall meet its blade in time."

Ahmetz had been right in one thing; his actions ended the fight. Order and Chaos were now so busy punishing Justice that they no longer cared if Eyso and D'alor were together. In the end, Ahmetz was fittingly punished: he was banished from judging the dead. Grandfather offered Ershk-gula a seat in the house of Order, which she accepted. She was given domain of the underworld, as fit her nature. It is her duty to know the end of all things, and to usher the dead to their final rest.

WINTER COMES TO EYSAN

By Dex Greenbright

In sparsely populated Irenorn, the tribes have a rich oral history. This, I think, is because there are so few trees and thus, no paper. When I went to see how the Northern Reach had fared in the plague (Some villages had not even heard of it! Imagine!), I was delighted to hear a story I had never come across before. Their view of the trickster god is somehow both more terrifying and sweeter than the myths I grew up with. I'm going to write it just as it was told to me. To transcribe it into a more formal myth wouldn't be true to its Irenorn legacy.

- Liridon MaRaukna

For quite a long time, the Dark Lady was depressed. She filled the dark rivers of the underworld with tears. Now, the other gods were all too afraid to do anything about it. Everywhere Ershk-gula went, death followed. The gods wondered if their immortality was really so strong against that strange and terrible power.

The only one who wasn't afraid was Ananya the trickster. He feared nothing and nobody. He saw the dark, sad pools of her eyes and was awestruck. Her grace in the face of her terrible duty fascinated him. Ananya was never given any duties for long, not ones he kept anyway. But he adored the Dark Lady, and wished above all things for her to find happiness. He made it his life's goal to bring a smile to her face.

He put on a disguise and traveled from the land of the gods and into Eysan. There he found a great feast. The trickster loved a good feast - all that chaotic drinking, fighting, loving, how could he not, yeh? The celebrators welcomed the stranger and unknowingly shared their food and drink with a god.

Ananya spent three days feasting with the mortals, out of respect for their generosity, but attending a party was never his intention. On the third night, he whispered lies to the group's spiritual leaders, promising all manner of wealth and glory if they sacrificed their followers.

The spiritual leaders, too drunk and blinded by Ananya's charm, took up their sacrificial knives. The feast ended in a bloodbath. When the leaders realized what they had done, they took their own lives as well. Ananya waited with the spirits of the celebrators. Before long, Ershk-gula arrived to collect them.

Ananya bowed low when he saw the Dark Lady and said, "I've made this gift for you, Ershk-gula. Fresh spirits, cut at the peak of life. Tell me they please you."

The Dark Lady frowned in response.

"Foolish trickster," she said, "I have thousands upon thousands of souls just like these."

She left with the souls, as it was her duty, but she remained as sad as ever.

Ananya didn't let it bother him. He vowed to find something another way to make Death smile.

He walked the length and breadth of Eysan, wondering what would make Ershk-gula happy. He had misjudged the problem, or rather, never considered it. Ananya isn't much of a sit-and-thinker, yeh? But he made a vow and he was going to keep it.

Perhaps, he thought, she could not see her beauty? The other gods were disgusted by her because of their fear. If the Dark Lady believed them, she might be blind to those very things that made her beautiful to the trickster. He knew then he needed the mirror of Yaim'allelo.

While many fear the goddess of the underworld, like they fear their own deaths, it is shifting Yaim'allelo who smart folks fear. The waters of Eysan are treacherous; only the brave and stupid make their livings upon the deep. But as dangerous as the shifting one is, everyone agrees Yaim'allelo is strikingly beautiful. Yaim'allelo knows this too. He-she keeps a magical mirror that reveals all beautiful things.

Ananya walked into the ocean. He found Water swimming gracefully amidst a school of glimmering fish of all colors.

"Esteemed one, how dull it is I find you here," he said.

Yaim'allelo stopped his-her swimming, surprised, and asked "Where else would I be?"

"Why, above the waves of your domain. Isn't that obvious?"

"What good would my father's domain be to me? It is far too dry, and the wind howls." he-she scoffed.

Ananya hid his smile, for he knew he had Yaim'allelo now. He merely said, "But oh great one of the current! when the waves are calm, and D'alor's eye shines bright, your realm becomes an even greater magical mirror than your small trinket in the sand there."

Yaim'allelo eyed the trickster.

"Impossible," he-she said, "There is only one mirror like that in the world."

"No?" Ananya cooed, "Let us go up together and I will prove that your ocean is a thousand times what your small mirror claims to be."

And so, Yaim'allelo and Ananya rose to the surface. The water was placid, and their reflections were indeed brilliant, but not magical.

The Shifting One held up his-her magic mirror and said, "You are wrong, little nephew. This is the only magic mirror."

Ananya smiled as he pointed to the ocean. "Look again," he said, "Truly see what is there."

55

When Yaim'allelo turned to see, the trickster god used his own magic to force images to appear on the surface. So enthralled was the shifting one, he-she did not notice the water itself was not the source.

"I had no idea my domain contained such power!" He-she said.

"It reflects both your beauty and strength, it seems," Ananya said, "but what of your small mirror? It's no use to you, when you can simply come here any time."

Yaim'allelo pushed the magic mirror toward Ananya without even looking, saying, "Perhaps you can find a use for it. A gift, for you to think of me by."

Ananya bowed and took the mirror. Then he disappeared, transporting himself to the gates of Ershk-gula's domain and leaving Yaim'allelo staring at the visions Ananya created on the surface of the ocean.

The trickster called for Ershk-gula in a loud and very pleased-with-himself voice. When the Dark Lady came to see what the fuss was about, Ananya presented her with the mirror.

"Your beauty may be different from some of those other gods, but you should love who you are," he said.

Ershk-gula stared into the mirror. Then she handed it back, tears in her dark eyes.

"Foolish trickster," she said, "I already accept myself. It is the world that does not accept me. The dead are no company, for their minds are filled with memories, the living fear me, as do my own kin. For good reason. I cannot even enjoy my mother's creations by walking the surface. I would kill everything by merely going for a stroll. Please, just go, and leave me to my duties."

Ananya finally understood. He knew what he must do to cheer up the goddess he realized he loved. He kissed Ershk-gula's hand in farewell before she returned to the underworld. She did not realize, but he had taken a small portion of her power.

He first went to Eyso, asking her to strengthen the plants against hardship. Then he went to D'alor to request he visit other lands for a time, and to take Zia-novalla, lady of Fire, with him. When these things were done, the land began growing cold.

Ananya then took the bit of Death's power, combined with his own tricks, and made the plants and animals sleep while he created something new. He drew droplets of water from the air and froze them into snow and ice. He decorated the land with these. It was as harsh and beautiful as he found the Dark Lady to be.

When the whole of Eysan was blanketed in white, he called once more for the Dark Lady.

Ershk-gula saw what Ananya had made for her. Not a single blade of grass died as she stepped upon the snow. She wept with joy. Ananya thought he had done something wrong, and was about to unmake his gift, but the Dark Lady stopped him. Her weeping turned to laughter.

"My dear trickster," she said with a smile, "This is the most beautiful thing I have ever seen."

The two were wed a short time after. They visit Eysan every year to celebrate their strange courtship, creating winter to protect the land from Death's power when they do.

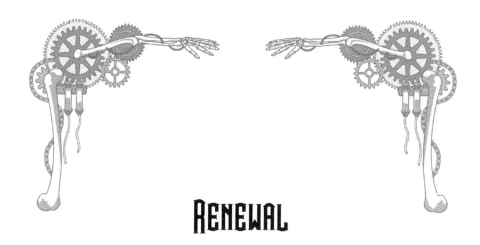

RENEWAL

By Victoria Bitters

There are a scant few scholars and historians who have had the unique opportunity to live on the secluded island nation of Homanoah. I actually met Master Historian Satrakks personally. They were hired to translate the Renewal myth into Shunniran by a university professor of Eysan studies. They confided that the copy made with footnotes and taken back to Eysan would have them barred from ever setting foot on Homanoah again. It's fuzzy whether I am committing a crime myself by copying it down. My only wish is to protect worldly knowledge from being lost and forgotten. May the Great Devourer and his people please forgive me if I have offended them in doing so.

- Liridon MaRaukna

The natural life cycle of one who pleases Ko'mo is this:

Born a child, grow into a man, bend with age into a salamander.

Now, you will see many these days who bend with age and do *not* transform into a lithe, plump shape, nimble and free, honored by all Homanoahns. Many men spend their whole lives and enter their deaths in the same skin. In this age, few have pleased Ko'mo as they once did, that He would give them another lifetime in a favored form – truly living as His children.

But once, all men could become salamanders. **[1]**

In the days of Keahkawen, there was a man who fed the fires of Ko'mo dutifully. He pledged himself to the Great Salamander's will and honored the pillars of His might – obedience, community, purity, and appetite. **[2]**

But as the years passed, he felt himself hampered in his devotion by his body's failures. The ashes of the holy fire chafed his skin and irritated his breathing. The spark of Ko'mo's great flame that He granted to all His people sank low within the man, and he mourned its banking. **[3]**

One day, the man journeyed to the highest peak of Oakalwilko, to make his final obeisance to the Great Devourer.

As the aged man made his way up the rough path, he saw movement in the shadows along the way. A small salamander was keeping pace with him. The man correctly saw this as a sign that the Great Salamander was welcoming him, but did not presume to think that the he was in the presence of Ko'mo himself. **[4]**

"Ah, favored brother, how I envy you. You are made in the image of the God, but I miss the days when I could see the similarities between us all the better. I miss possessing plump, rounded skin, taut with the glow of youth."

The small salamander flowed over the hard rocks beside the man, fluid like the first rush of lava. The man sighed.

"I miss the days when I could run and climb, stretch and bend, nights when I could sleep soundly on any surface."

The small salamander paused and tilted its head at the man. Encouraged by this magnanimous gesture, the man spoke on.

"Now I shiver in dried out skin that feels all the rough elements and holds in none of Ko'mo's blessed heat." The man sighed again and gestured respectfully to the small salamander.

"I can still serve His glory, but it is a great sorrow to me that I do not do so as well as I have done." The man hung his head, his sadness weighing upon him. **[5]**

Suddenly, the small salamander's shadow billowed and rose, buffeting and warming as it towered over the man. Fire fell from the patches of still visible sky that were His eyes. Heavy burning flecks of beneficent spittle lapped the earth around them. Thus was the presence of Ko'mo revealed.

In a voice that shook the earth, the Great Devourer spoke,

"YOU DO NOT LIKE YOUR FORM. THEN TAKE ANOTHER."

The God's holy words enveloped the man in a red warmth, and he fell into darkness, overcome. **[6]** When he next blinked open his eyes, he saw a much larger sky than he had ever known before, studded with brilliant, distant fires. He felt warm rock pleasantly beneath his hands and feet and belly. He breathed in air heavily laden with enticing scents. Tipping his head, he saw his worn, brown skin, was now a glossy, beautiful black. He felt joy and gratitude.

The once-man hurried over the distance back to his village, glorying in the speed Ko'mo had granted him. He stopped often to rest in the many shaded and damp havens that his neighbors had constructed for the shelter of small salamanders. He dined upon the plentiful nourishment that flourished in this, Ko'mo worldly paradise. **[7]**

When the once-man reached his old home, he danced a greeting to his neighbors who were passing by. Many stopped to admire his beauty and gesture respectfully to him. The once-man's eldest son squinted in awe as he began to suspect the truth.

"Does this small salamander not seem... familiar, to anyone else?"

Others who had known the once-man in his previous form began to nod slowly. The eldest son's eldest son held his hand to the small salamander and the once-man tapped the back of the young man's hand, instructively. **[8]**

The impressed gathering regarded the once-man as he proudly darted about, tracing the sign of Ko'mo on the stone before his front door.

An old woman who had grown up with the man gasped and cried out, "I recognize that sinuous saunter, from days long past! This is our recent neighbor! The man we knew, in new skin!" **[9]**

The people quickly summoned a priestess to witness the miracle. Given great insight by the Devourer Himself, the priestess was able to explain to the once-man's family and neighbors how he came to be transformed.

Many thanks were offered to the God and all who saw the once-man in his beautiful new shape re-dedicated themselves to Ko'mo with ever greater passion, that they too might one day earn his blessing.

[1] This is not meant to imply that followers of Ko'mo may ascend to gods themselves, as Ko'mo does in the myths by 'devouring' the gods of the east. Their spirits remain lowly and mortal, they simply are granted a "do over" in a form that has considerably fewer responsibilities than a man possesses.

[2] The fourth meritorious element of Homanoahn society can be interpreted as 'yearning for the unattained', 'desire for improvement', or simply 'willingness to eat whatever one is fed'.

[3] The idea of a god-granted 'spark within' as both a driving force, embodying life and ambition, and a blessing and confirmation of the god's favor is a sentiment shared by some Eastern worshippers. One would presume followers of Ko'mo would find kinship with followers of Zia-novella but it seems the only similarities between those two groups of adherents is their willingness to engage in fire fights.

[4] Though never specifically outlined as a virtue, "appropriate" humility is often lauded in Homanoahn lessons. This appropriateness is determined by relative rank. All Homahnoans are implicitly urged to consider themselves superior to all non-Homahnoans, for example.

[5] Homanoahn society has rigid views on a job well done. A colloquialism that alarms many a newcomer translates literally to "If you can't do it correctly, burn away your failure." Those who have acclimatized to the idioms of the culture take this as an expression of high standards. Those who have actually lived here for any period of time may notice that there are in fact a fair number of 'crimes of incompetence', the perpetrators of which are sentenced to death by volcanic vent.

[6] It is commonly understood that this scene is a description of the final eruption of Oakalwilko – Ko'mo's Angry Voice - in the eighth year of the Naa age. Given the focus of this lesson, the narrative necessarily glosses over resulting deaths and hardships experienced by the untransformed locals.

[7] Homahnoans believe that their island is the best possible place to foster life, disregarding the poisonous plants and animals, questionable soil for standard crops, and frequent eruptions and earth-shakes from their volcanoes. One is not sure how to take the assurance that the god known as the Great Devourer's *spiritual* paradise is "even better".

[8] The 'eldest son's eldest son' is a common role in Homanoahn lessons – the existence of the character signifies the fertility of generations, while the actions of the character indicate the ignorance of youth being literally struck down – and thus conquered – when one respectfully applies to a senior for correction. Typically, the 'instructive tap' is more of a hearty slap, but the relative weakness of a salamander inadvertently makes this into a gentle scene between generations.

[9] I cannot get the younger novices to stop pronouncing this line as "in **newt** skin". It is very annoying.

TRICKSTER'S CRAFT

By Dex Greenbright

This myth is the life's work of Archivist Beatrice Mathille. The original tale was lost when the Haakon Republic was in its infancy. Pieces survived as what was remembered was told and retold. Beatrice scoured every Library in the land for these scraps of lore. She compiled her findings into a book of forgotten myths. It is not only the story of many gods' creation, but also the story that would become the Trickster's Hand game.

- Liridon MaRaukna

When the universe was young, the gods of Chaos lived separately from those of Order. Being intensely curious, Ontaakh often wondered who these rigid, unimaginative beings were on the other side of creation, and why they were so hated. He had been rebuffed by Order before, when Ahmetz the Just was created to stop him. But Ontaakh could not leave a mystery unsolved. He snuck across the divide, to learn all he could about these enemies.

Ontaakh took in all he encountered and wrote his observations on scrolls he kept in a large knapsack. He discovered a stretch of solid ground covered in all manner of plants, animals, and mortals, but there were no gods in sight. He came upon a volcano spewing great plumes of smoke into the air. He followed a river of burning lava up to the crater at the very summit. He took a fall halfway up and cursed as his little finger became one with the red flow. He used his godly power to grow a replacement of iron and continued on his journey. Near the top, his footing slipped and he lost several toes to the lava. Again he cried out, and again a replacement grew forth -- this time of gold.

When the god of knowledge reached the top, he was surprised to be greeted by a statuesque goddess. Her skin was the color of clay, and green vines were interwoven in her hair. Her flowing dress was a pastiche of flowers, grasses, and leaves, with slate ornaments.

Ontaakh kept his distance.

"Are you a daughter of Order?"

The goddess nodded.

"I am Eyso. And you, little god?"

"Ontaakh. You are not as Chaos described."

Eyso smiled warmly. She ignored the comment, and gestured to the landscape.

"Have you enjoyed your wanderings?"

"I have learned much. Truly, these are fascinating lands you maintain. It surprised me that one of Grandfather's written children could stand such varied beauty."

"But of course. I am life embodied."

Ontaakh paused a moment before coming to realize the weight of the goddess's words. She *was* the land he had been traveling.

Just then, two small figures emerged from the volcano. The taller child was Ro'ag the Harbinger. He dragged a massive sword behind him that was as iron gray as his armored skin. The shorter child was Zia-novalla the Bright. She was a thin wisp of a girl who glowed a warm gold and whose eyes were small pools of fire.

The young gods strode up to their elders and addressed them as mother and father.

64

Ontaakh was horrified. How had such a thing occurred?

Eyso pointed to the lava flows where he had lost his finger and toes.

"You gave your flesh to me. I could do little else but create. It is my way."

Ontaakh begged the goddess to forgive his terrible intrusion. She insisted all was forgiven, but warned that Chaos and Order would never allow the children to live if discovered. The god of knowledge then thought of a way to hide the young deities from both sides.

On his way back to Chaos, he took a scroll from his knapsack and unfurled it between two sides of the universe. Eyso sprinkled some of her life-giving earth onto the scroll, creating a new vibrant world for the two young gods.

Back in the ever-changing land of Chaos, Ontaakh met with his brother. D'alor was fascinated by the description of the goddess and her land of plants and animals. Before long, the god of the sky soared across the border to meet Eyso.

D'alor flew above Eyso's land, bringing the sun and rain in his wake. At first, Eyso was frustrated by his presence, but then realized how the god's gifts enhanced her creations. She saw in him a wondrous brightness and he saw in her imagination and tenderness beyond measure. A more natural pairing had never been seen, nor ever might again.

The two were bound together in a great storm. Born of this tumultuous coupling were Yaim'allelo of the Deep and Alillia the Tranquil. Sky and Land loved one another dearly, and wished to keep their children close, but feared Chaos and Order's wrath as Ontaakh had.

The new deities were sent to live in the between world with their half-siblings War and Fire until Eyso and D'alor could find a way that all could live together in safety if not harmony.

The four children lived happily for a time, but quickly became bored, as children do. They were playing in the dirt when Alillia appealed to her brother-sister for help.

"Yaim'allelo, use your powers to make clay, that we may create more friends to play with."

The Shifting One agreed, and formed a pool that would turn the dirt into sculpting clay. The young deities used the gift of life they received from their mother to craft small animals to befriend. Zia-novalla molded a winged serpent and placed within it a portion of her very own fire. Ro'ag made a wolf with iron teeth that would hunt with him. Alillia sculpted many small birds to sing with. Yaim'allelo crafted a turtle with a shimmering rainbow shell to ride upon. Then the Bright One used her powers to warm and set the forms of the clay animals, bringing them to life.

The children loved their pets dearly, but soon grew bored again. A beast cannot play in the same way a god can. So the children worked together to sculpt a friend in their image. War gave the clay god strength, Peace gave playfulness, and Fire gave cleverness. Water was worried that if this new playmate were to ally himself with Chaos or Order, he would no longer wish to play with the young deities, so he-she put a shifting nature into the clay.

When this new god was baked into life, he was indeed strong, playful, clever, with no allegiance. He danced in a mad circle, much to the delight of all. The new god finished by jumping up in the air and hanging upside down from a tree. He bowed up toward his dangling legs with a wry grin.

"Greetings, small creators. I am Ananya!"

The young deities gleefully shouted for Ananya to join them in play. But they could not agree on what they would do.

Ananya flew down from the tree to stop their arguing.

"We should go exploring. There are two fine worlds out there beyond the borders."

Zia-novalla protested.

"And how would we do that? We cannot leave, lest Grandmother and Grandfather find us."

"A riddle for me? Aha, and I know just how to solve it!"

In the blink of an eye, he gathered the young deities into his hand which became a magic satchel. Then, he cut his arm and bled on the dirt. Ananya turned himself into a beetle whose shell shimmered in all colors. When great Eyso peered through the barrier, she saw the blood on the ground.

66

Thinking her children had come to great harm, she screamed so loud it could be heard in the farthest corners of the universe.

The elder gods pierced the borders of chaos and order. Grandfather Q'ua charged toward Eyso's cry, ready to defend his daughter. His magic pen lengthened into a formidable spear. At the same moment, Grandmother Rau-cilla rushed in with her golden sword, recognizing the cry of a mother. Before either saw Eyso, Ananya took her into his satchel as well, for it would not do to spoil the trick too early. Q'ua and Rau-cilla met on the blood-soaked clearing, each accusing the other of terrible things.

Ananya cleared his tiny, beetle throat.

"Grandfather and Grandmother of the universe, why do you quarrel so?"

Rau-cilla looked down, but she could not see the small trickster. So Ananya grabbed the satchel and flew up to rest on her shoulder. When Grandmother spied him, she pursed her lips. Her golden sword hovered just above his carapace.

"What magic is this? What manner of god are you? What have you done with Eyso?"

"Oh no, Grandmother! I am a mere animal. I would do nothing to harm Eyso. She is alive and well."

"How is it that you speak, then, beetle?"

"All of us animals can do so, when we are so inclined. But here, I did not call you to discuss speaking."

Rau-cilla narrowed her gaze.

"You called us?"

"With Eyso's help, yes. I have gifts in this satchel to honor each of you, Great Ones."

Q'ua thrust the butt of his spear to the ground.

"I accept your gifts, so long as my gifts are greater, as Order is more valuable than Chaos."

Rau-cilla glowered and the air grew thunderous around her.

"Without Chaos there would be nothing but empty space. I am deserving of more than this fool."

Ananya lifted his forelegs in a placating gesture.

"Before you divvy your gifts, allow me to first give you a small taste."

He reached into the satchel to retrieve four bright baubles. He lifted them for Q'ua to inspect. The green one was the calm and steadfastness of Alillia. The blue one was the rhythmic ebb and flow of Yaim'allelo's waters. The red one was the strict tactics of battle. The yellow one was the inevitability of fire. Q'ua was indeed pleased, but before he could take his gifts, Ananya returned them to the satchel.

It was then Rau-cilla's turn to see what she might receive. She was shown the unpredictability of love in green, tumultuous waters in blue, the passion of red, and the dancing light of yellow. Her smile warmed the space between realms. But again, Ananya hid the prizes back within the satchel.

The trickster presented the satchel to the first gods.

"Since you gods know far more than a mere animal, I shall give the entire satchel to the both of you. Divide it how you deem fair."

They attempted to open the satchel, but were denied. They grew furious.

Ananya bowed so low, his carapace nestled into the dirt.

"I do apologize, great ones. I forgot, the bag is mine and tied to me. You will need to cut it in two. Each gets the contents of a half."

The gods did not hesitate. They attacked the satchel, hoping for the prizes within. Ananya was in a blinding pain, for despite the magics he used to create the satchel out of his hand, he still felt every hit. Such is the power of the first gods and a power the trickster planned for. But, the first gods could never have planned for Ananya.

The trickster moved quickly to protect Eyso and the young deities from unintended harm. He also moved the gods to separate areas of the bag, so he alone knew which would end up where. When the satchel was severed, it once again turned into Ananya's hand and in the same instant he returned

68

to his natural form. The five fingers of his left hand had all been cut off. Standing in Q'ua's portion were Alillia and Eyso. Rau-cilla received Yaim'allelo, Ro'ag, and Zia-novalla.

Furious and confused, Q'ua grabbed Ananya by the neck.

"What is this? You give me my own creation? And what are these others? They are gods! As are you!"

"Your gift is indeed greater, as you requested. And Grandmother's is more plentiful."

The first gods began to argue once more. They demanded answers from anyone who would dare speak. While they raged and threatened one and all, Ananya used his trickster magic to craft new fingers out of the rainbow carapace of his beetle form. When he was done, he addressed Q'ua and Rau-cilla.

"You both wish to have everything. I know a way you can have it just so." He paused, grinning. "Join your realms together."

Q'ua huffed and Rau-cilla raged, but they responded the same.

"Impossible!"

Ananya laughed at them.

"You are two sides of one universe. Parts of each of you lie in all of creation, written by Q'ua or spoken by Rau-cilla. If you were so distant, why would you possibly want all of these young gods for your own?"

The first gods looked at one another and knew the trickster's words to be true. In their great mercy, they spared the lived of the young gods and Ananya. The feud of the first gods ended that very day and the barrier between Chaos and Order was torn down.

The World of Eysan

HOMANOAH

LEGEND
Mountains
Ocean / Sea
Marshland
Desert
Swamp Forest
Canyon
Volcano
River
Capital City

Perragrox Mountains

Trenorn

Kalahn Sea

Teraltis

Shunnira

Ukketia

Fiu Mountains

Beskra

Eastern Desert (Lobhi)

Djimbur

Aadobur

70

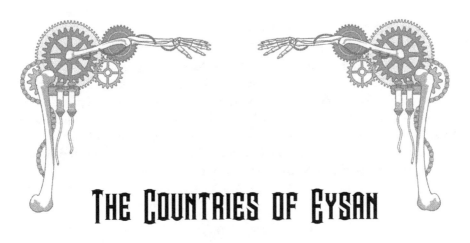

The Countries of Eysan

From the notes of Liridon MaRaukna

Teraltis

Teraltis is the biggest country by area, and growing steadily larger by the day. How is this possible, you ask? After the fall of the Haakon Republic, when borders were being drawn, the Teraltians convinced the Aadoburi to mark the divide between them at the eastern edge of the desert. Unfortunately for my people, the Eastern Desert (Lobhi to the Aadoburi and the Nomadic tribes who call the desert home) has been expanding, devouring the fertile farmlands of Aadobur ever since.

The Teraltians are ruled by Emperor Falkoun the Great, supported by a council of advisors selected from the nobility. The latter has been gaining power over the past century, and perform many of the smaller, day to day tasks required of ruling an empire.

Religion can mean many things to a Teraltian. Typically, a family will choose a patron god to worship from the pantheon. Since the royal family's god is D'alor, many citizens worship him as well. I would dare guess this is the reason so many see the sky as the future, and why the floating cities are so popular.

Separated from the rest of Teraltis by the Itu Mountains, the Nomads who roam the desert never integrated their culture with those of the west and north. They have strict rules in place for safety and social interaction.

One thing which can be confusing to outsiders is the concept of a name that changes based on one's status. Every Nomad begins with a childhood name given to them by their parents. Tradition dictates it have five letters. Those who have high ranking within their society, whether by reputation or profession, are allowed to drop letters from their name. Tribe leaders have one-letter names. Outcasts might have as many as eight. Nomads are known as the inventors of the first airship, and pilots are highly respected. I had the honor of meeting a Nomad pilot with a two-letter name.

Shunnira

Much as Teraltians are known for their arrogance and prying into the lives of all on Eysan, Shunnirans have a reputation for being relaxed, creative, and friendly. I must say that on the whole, I've found this to be true. Of course, every individual is different, but the variety of unique and wonderful people I've met there has always astounded me. And if you ever have the opportunity, I recommend you try Shunniran coffee.

Shunnira is the biggest country by population and is overseen by an elected council which rules as an oligarchy for a period of a decade before new elections must take place. Official census-takers are sent out at that time to count citizens and collect votes.

My favorite location within Shunnira is the Beskra Canyonlands. This sparse landscape is home to the Grand Library of Ontaakh, which houses the largest collection of knowledge in all of Eysan. It is home to the Order of Scholars (and has been my home for several years as I've trained to become a Historian of the Order).

Some northerners have the mistaken belief that Djimbuk is a separate country, or even stranger to me, a myth! While Djimbuk is separated from the continent by a wide channel, it is nonetheless an integral part of Shunniran industry and home to its most famous university. While most cities lie along the coast, a few have been constructed deep in the rainforest. I've only seen one, but it was a marvel of engineering. The buildings wrap around living trees, with elevators and bridges connecting the structures. Glider technology has been perfected here; fliers routinely maneuver through the canopy.

Aadobur

The country of my birth is steeped in tradition. You can see it in the architecture, which attempts to preserve Haak designs where it can, and replicate them where it cannot. It is the country that follows the old religious traditions most closely. And the culture of the Aadoburi is one of strict responsibilities to family and country.

Aadobur is split into several hierarchical classes, with the bureaucrats at the top and homeless and outcasts at the bottom. There are few ways to gain standing, but many ways one can lose it. My situation is unusual, in that I was taken in from the streets by an upper noble family. While my official class never changed, I was given opportunities similar to those of my adopted class.

While there is technically peace between Aadobur and Teraltis, it is a poorly hidden fact that soldiers patrol the border on both sides and have small skirmishes on occasion. Despite this, Aadobur is a launching point for many would-be treasure hunters. They sneak across the border into Lobhi (Eastern Desert) to search the Haak ruins for relics. Many Aadoburi nobles collect any and all things from ancient Haakon. Because of the danger and rareness of these items, forgeries are common.

The Floating Cities

The floating cities have been a major advancement in mechanics, launching humanity skyward. They would not be possible without the dedicated work of the aethericists who discovered and developed new marvelous gases into the fuel for these amazing feats of engineering.

Many who understand how they function will argue until blue in the face that the cities do not *actually* float, but fly and hover. But from the ground, the cities appear to glide gracefully over the landscape on a bed of clouds. They are truly stunning to behold.

Dantus was the first of the floating cities to be made. It was conceived as a luxury destination for the wealthy nobles of Teraltis. Some nobles constructed vacation homes there, but the technology was not yet trusted by many and space was eventually sold to wealthy families of Shinnura and Aadobur as well.

Once Dantus was considered a success, everyone wanted to spend time aboard a floating city. Emperor Falkoun was particularly smitten with the idea and commissioned a new, mobile capital for Teraltis. Caelspyr is the largest of the floating cities.

Kibou was the brainchild of the Inventors and Artificers Guilds. They moved both guild headquarters to Caelspyr, but the safety of the Emperor forced most of their experiments to be conducted elsewhere. Kibou was to house many workshops, a university, and a vast network of supply shops.

The plague caused many to flee to the safety of the skies. All three floating cities quickly became laden with refugees. There were several other, smaller floating cities built, though they were eventually abandoned and the resources incorporated into Caelspyr and Kibou, creating bustling communities for all people of Eysan aboard the cities. I cannot begin to imagine how much extra fuel is required to keep these cities aloft now!

In my travels, I have heard many people voice their opinions o the floating cities. Dantus is seen as a business hub, Kibou as a center for industry, and Caelspyr is considered either a foreboding shadow of imperial meddling or a vault of wealth and opportunity.

Homanoah

The island country of Homanoah is largely shrouded in mystery. Trade with outsiders is limited, and carefully controlled by the Homanoahn government. Only a select few citizens of the continent countries have been allowed to keep residence over the years. They are typically Scholars and other people deemed useful to Homanoahn society. What little knowledge we have about the island is from their accounts.

Homanoah is a theocracy, led by a high priestess. She is known to disappear into the depths of her mountain temple for days at a time to confer with the Homanoahn deity Ko'mo about matters of state.

Ko'mo, the sole god of the Homanoahns, is a mystical salamander the size of a mountain. He's said to live inside the largest of the country's volcanoes. In Homanoahn legend, there were once many gods (and this includes the gods of the Haakon Republic worshiped on the mainland), but Ko'mo - in a display of power and mighty hunger - ate them. Difficult to even imagine, I know. How would a land creature, no matter how godly, possibly hope to fight Grandmother Rau-cilla who embodies chaos itself?

RELIGION OF THE CONTINENT
- A PRIMER ON THE GODS -

From the notes of Liridon MaRaukna

It often amazes me how little people know of the gods they believe in. Our knowledge of the gods comes from the Haak and has varied little from the end of the Haakon Republic. Growing up Aadoburi myself, I was taught to mind all the gods equally. But many of Eysan follow only one deity, and are ignorant of all others. This is how I typically teach the basics to those who ask. Yes, I am aware this is not typically a duty for a historian, especially one who is agnostic at best, but how can I stand idly while there is knowledge to be shared?

Chaos, Order, and the beginning of all things

The first two gods were Grandmother Rau-cilla and Grandfather Q'ua. Chaos and Order. In the time before being, the two were constantly at odds. As chaos is forever restless, one day Rau-cilla sang the sky into being and called him D'alor. Jealous of Grandmother's creation, Q'ua took his pen and wrote the land into being and named her Eyso.

Grandmother Chaos could not understand Q'ua, and her wildness refused to give her peace until she knew why Order was so different from

76

herself. And so, she spoke Ontaakh - the patron god of my Order - into being. The god of knowledge tried to comprehend the divide between Order and Chaos. Q'ua in turn wrote Ahmetz, god of justice, to life to stop what must never be known.

Those four gods - land and sky, knowledge and justice - were the only directly created by Grandmother Chaos and Grandfather Order. The remaining gods - those of fire, water, war, peace, business, fate, the afterlife, and the trickster god – sprung from the four children of Chaos and Order.

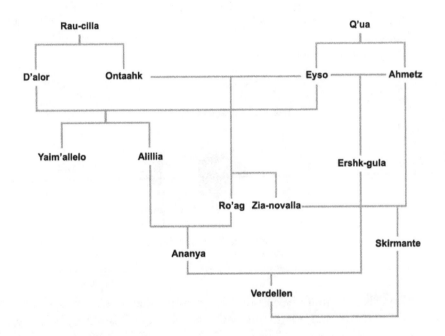

Rau-cilla

Also called Grandmother, Chaos, or both together, Rau-cilla is one of the original two gods. She embodies change and chaos. Her powerful Children all carry some aspect of her. Rau-cilla's form of creation is verbal – she sings or speaks her ideas into reality.

Q'ua

Also called Grandfather, Order, or both together, Q'ua is the other of the original two gods. He embodies stability and order. His stalwart Children reflect aspects of him, as Children of Chaos do of her. Q'ua creates with the steady stroke of his mighty quill, writing his thoughts into being.

D'alor

Many families choose a patron god to align themselves to. The Teraltian imperial family is no different, though when such a powerful family chooses a patron god, it has national consequences. They wanted a powerful symbol of the burning brightness they wished to mark upon the world. The god of the sky and daytime fit perfectly. His watchful eye is the sun. Some suggest that the floating cities were created to curry favor with D'alor, to keep his followers safe from the plague. D'alor is also the chosen god of those who sail the skies.

Eyso

The goddess of the land, the harvest, life, and creation has the most followers among farmers and others who work the land. Though not divine, we are her children, too, as she supports and feeds us. Stories told by the followers of Eyso focus on her generosity and how much she encompasses. She is the source of life and the progenitor of death.

Ontaakh

The god of knowledge is, of course, my patron god. The Order of Scholars has created their temples to be vast libraries and schools. I may have to make an entire entry on my beloved Order. Why Ontaakh is not the most popular god in all creation is entirely beyond me. Without sharing information and a curiosity about the world, humanity as we know it would not exist!

Though historically, Ontaakh is described as in opposition to the god of justice, it can also be argued that without one, the other would never have come to be. Without understanding, how can one hope to build a fair framework for the rules by which we live?

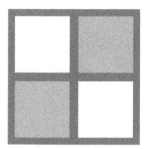

Ahmetz

Ah, the god of justice. Patron of law enforcement, judges, and charities wishing to aid those that have been left behind by society. Justice is a lofty goal. Even the great god himself has faltered in many of the old stories, being too rigid to do any lasting good. Sometimes referred to as "The Unbending Arrow," this god is sometimes paired with Ro'ag. Their couplings can result in both precise victories and sprawling wrecks. Crude idioms exist to suggest that these outcomes are results of one or the other being, ahem, *dominant*, but I feel that the gods should be allowed their privacy as much as any of us, and will refrain from my own speculations.

Zia-novalla

Goddess of fire, daughter of Ontaakh and Eyso. Her realm ranges from the wild, molten fires of volcanoes to the bound and serviceable fires of the hearth. She is notably the patron of blacksmiths and is considered a co-patron, alongside her mother, to all those whose crafts cross into her realm: glassblowers and ceramicists, cooks, smelters, and chemists. She is treated with respect by those of my order, as she both grants the boon of light to read by and will consume any carelessly handled scroll or book.

Yaim'allelo

Some people shun the brother-sister of water, unable to comprehend the shifting nature of water. Calm and stormy, Shallow and deep, Tropical and Arctic, he-she surrounds us with his-her domain. Often described as unrelentingly beautiful and unforgiving, all those who work upon the waves are careful to beware Yaim'allelo's tumultuous side.

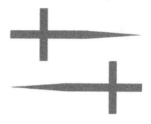

Ro'ag

Known as the Harbinger of War and the Iron One, Ro'ag is the god of battle and tactical thinking. Your soldiers and mercenaries will often choose Ro'ag as their patron, though many athletes also prefer him. He is also considered a god of love and passion, particularly when paired with Alillia or Ahmetz.

Alillia

The goddess of peace is often overlooked in favor of gods who represent things that effect one's everyday life (the sky, the land, water, fire), until one is injured or ill. Peace is the patron of medics and healers! Look next time and you'll see her crossed-petals symbol adorning the walls of your local hospital. She is also sometimes the favored goddess of soldiers who manage to retire, as well as being fervently invoked by new parents.

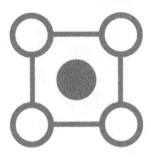

Skirmante

Another very popular goddess, Skirmante the Keen is the patron of wealth and business. Banks will often be led by a Purveyor of Skirmante (think of them like the Scholars of my Order or the Acolytes of Ershk-gula). Merchants of all kinds favor her as well.

Appropriately, Skirmante came into being as a result of a pragmatic deal between the gods of justice and fire. Ahmetz sought Zia-novalla's aid in purifying a set of scales so that no taint of bias might creep in. In exchange, the goddess requested one of Ahmetz's eyes. The price was steep, and Justice refused until Fire gave a demonstration of her power. She purified a single link in a chain, making it able to bear any weight. Ahmetz was immediately convinced and cut out his eye for her. She placed the eye upon one of the hanging plates and bathed the scales in molten light until they glowed as brightly as the sun. All the gods, save Zia-novalla herself, were forced to look away until the scales had cooled. None understood the smile upon Zia-novalla's face until the process was complete. When the purified scales had cooled, Skirmante stood perfectly balanced atop the fulcrum. Zia-novalla's true bargain with Ahmetz was for a daughter.

Those who have fallen afoul of unfair dealings or who are embroiled in large debts are sometimes referred to as "Skirmante's mules" and, in some places, may petition that she "redistribute their burdens." These petitions may range from practices as ephemeral as going through purifying rites, up to more practical negotiations for the "mule's" labor on behalf of Skirmante's order to substitute for debt installment payments.

Verdellen

Goddess of fate and the future, Verdellen is often invoked as one departs. "Go with Verdellen" or similar. It has been argued for centuries whether Verdellen has already decided the fate of all beings, or if her favor can be won and fates can be changed.

Dominant opinions of her adherents or individual temples may be deduced by the material they use to depict her symbols -- stone or metal would indicate the former opinion while wax or other pliant materials are clear signs of the latter. I've read a fascinating treatise by a sculptor on the subject with clay as the central analogy. Any idea can be reworked until it is fixed into place by the fires of action.

Verdellen and Skirmante as lovers enjoy a quiet, humble affection. Though creating no children of their own, the couple are seen as protectors of those in need of family including any shunned by their birth families, orphans, and lost pets. But do not fool yourself into thinking that love tames either goddess's power. Their coupling is seen as a divine partnership, building and playing off of one another. Praying to the couple is believed to bring about a future of good fortune and abundance. Whereas disrespecting *either* goddess invites punishment from both.

Ershk-gula

While devout followers of D'alor or Eyso often choose a funeral ceremony that keeps in line with their own practice, the dead ultimately belong to Ershk-gula. Many fear her, to the point that some stories cast her as a wicked, evil creature. She's one part psychopomp, leading the dead to their place of rest, and one part gentle caretaker to the souls in her domain.

Deserts are sometimes said to be places where "Ershk-gula has stood on every grain," though of course these regions are still of Eyso and, in fact, are often bustling with life in their own way. Winter is considered her season in the north, while summer is hers in the south. I don't have any information about when year-round temperate regions think she is prominent, but in truth and in my experience, all seasons welcome her in their own way.

Ananya

I struggle to believe the stories of any gods as strictly true. In my mind, they are helpful stories, explaining the world or human nature through a particular lens. I've been told that I am "Ananya-touched" because of this. The trickster god is essentially Chaos embodied: Grandmother's favorite.

Any who need creativity in their work or lives call upon Ananya for his blessing. I once read about rumors of a secret Order of spies and con artists who use Ananyan iconography and claim to be devout followers of the trickster, but I've never seen any evidence such a group exists.

There are many conflicting stories about Ananya and how the trickster god came to be. The version uncovered by Archivist Beatrice Mathille, where many gods participated, is the oldest known, but not the most popular. A sacred text of Rau-cilla reclaimed from a dusty Aadoburi temple basement claims that Grandmother Chaos sang Ananya's birth. Another tale alludes to lightning and rainbows but no direct creator, making the trickster as primordial as Chaos and Order. In one, he began as a mortal and became a god through his cunning. The most commonly accepted explanation is that he is the son of Alillia and Ro'ag.

Though even there, I've heard three different myths. In the first, Ro'ag and Alillia hid their hearts within a secret cave while they attempted to build trust between order and chaos. When they returned, the hearts had grown together. Ananya was what bound them. The second story is similar, but Ananya was in his beetle form and might have been a normal beetle before feasting on god-blood. The third tells of a young god born of a coupling not meant to be, where Ro'ag and Alillia cycled through arguments as often as the tides change.

The most baffling part of such widely varied stories is that the temples of Ananya make no effort to choose among the versions and instead officially claim *every* origin of Ananya to be true. And as more people realize this, new stories are told. I expect there will be five more officially accepted versions by the end of the year.

In most of the old stories, it was Ananya who finally bridged the two opposing forces of chaos and order. In fact, the trickster is often the one bringing forbidden knowledge to the world or to the gods. He uses guile to convince others to do what is ultimately the best solution.

The Order of Scholars

From the notes of Liridon MaRaukna

The Order of Scholars is the premier source of knowledge in all of Eysan. Our Order does not have as much ritual or worship as many other Orders, but our members are nevertheless passionate about what our patron god represents: information, wisdom, and knowledge. The temples of Ontaakh are libraries, schools, and museums as well as places of worship. In times of crisis, scholars are consulted for solutions.

There are three paths for a member of the Order to follow: scholar, historian, and archivist. Each plays an important role in the Order. But a new member does not need to decide immediately which path they will take.

Levels Within the Order

One begins in the Order of Scholars as a potential. It's a sort of introductory stage, where scholars test the potential's desire to study and protect the collective knowledge of the world. A potential's job is to learn, both about the world and about the Order. University attendance and a donation to the temple in the form of a book or artifact is recommended. Advancement occurs after completion of a written test.

Next, one becomes a novice. Novices are given small tasks around a temple and spend time assisting masters of all three paths, shadowing them in their duties and performing small, administrative tasks. This period lasts for a minimum of a year, but can be longer. It ends when the novice chooses a path for themself.

Once on a path, the novice becomes an associate. Associates continue working and studying and are generally given the most grueling tasks. Advancement to the level of adept relies on a completed thesis related to one's path. This often takes five or more years.

Many members of the Order spend years, even decades, as an adept. This is when we hone our skills and do the most good for both the Order and the world. Many teachers and doctors are adept scholars. Adept historians are the ones who travel the most, seeking to build upon the knowledge preserved by the Order. Adept archivists are tasked with temple upkeep and improvements. One only advances to master when they have made a significant contribution to the Order or the world and have been approved by the masters of their path. Traditionally, one remains an adept for a period of at least ten years.

The highest level one can achieve within the Order of Scholars is that of master. Masters are highly respected for their wisdom and experience. These are leaders of the temples and advisors to world leaders. This level is hard to achieve. Some members have dedicated their whole life to the Order on their way to becoming a master. They wear their metal-threaded symbols of Ontaakh with pride.

It is my dearest hope that one day someone will read these notes and become inspired to join. Below, I will describe a little about each of the paths within the Order.

Scholars

The public face of the Order, scholars are teachers, doctors, political advisors, and do the administrative work of running the temples. Typically the master scholar with the longest tenure in a temple is considered the top authority on internal matters. Scholars wear the symbol of Ontaakh in yellow or gold thread.

Historians

Without historians, every temple of Ontaakh would be an empty building. We travel the world, seeking knowledge. Sometimes this means collecting books and artifacts. Most of the time, we listen and write down the living history of the world and its people. Some historians are gifted with messenger falcons (it was my great privilege and pleasure to be counted among that number). Historians wear the symbol in orange or copper.

Archivists

The third path of the Order (and one that is vitally important to the Temples) are the archivists. They are caretakers of the temples and its spiritual leaders. When a book must be copied from handwriting to printed type, you will find an archivist heading the project. If worshippers come in to pray, an archivist will perform the service. Archivists wear the symbol in blue or silver.

THE GUILDS

From the notes of Liridon MaRaukna

Whereas orders are groups of like-minded individuals who follow the teachings and aspects of a particular god, guilds are organizations made up of people who excel within a scientific field or are masters of crafting particular machines. There are several guilds, but most often I have encountered the two most prominent guilds: the Artificers Guild and the Inventors Guild.

Artificers Guild

Artificers gather and make materials to later be used by the inventors or to sell directly to merchant factories across the continent. If you need a part or a resource, an artificer can help you get it. Within the Artificers, you will find sub-guilds for:

- **Smelters** excel in all forms of metalcraft.

- **Extractors** are mining and demolitions experts.

- **Crafters** design and make machine parts.

Inventors Guild

I would venture that everyone on Eysan has heard of the Inventors Guild, sometimes simply called "the Guild." They are highly lauded across the continent, though that reputation has tarnished some. Those who are disgruntled or distrustful of the Inventors call them tinkerers as an insult. Within the Inventors Guild you will find these sub-guilds:

- **Inventors** lead the guild, procure materials, head major cross-guild projects such as was needed to create the Automazombs.

- **Engineers** build most of the machinery we have come to depend on in our modern times. Locomotives, the floating cities, and, yes, the Automazombs.

- **Mechanics** take charge of machines after they are built, running and maintaining them. They're considered a sub-guild of engineers.

- **Chemists** create a variety of liquids and powders ranging from fuels, to medicines, to the lifeblood of the Automazombs.

- **Aethericists** are experts in all manner of gases, but are now revered for their recent developments in floating cities and airships.

- **Hydraulicists** are the geniuses of pumps, irrigation, and water-cleaning systems.

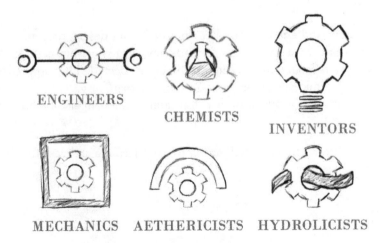

ENGINEERS

CHEMISTS

INVENTORS

MECHANICS   AETHERICISTS   HYDROLICISTS

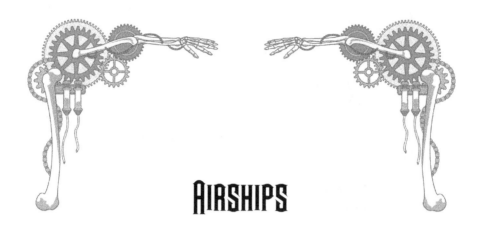

AIRSHIPS

From the notes of Liridon MaRaukna

Airships of varying sizes have long been an important component of our lives. But many are unaware of the origin of these vehicles and the variety of sizes and shapes one might see. Having traveled the continent for several years now, I have seen a great many and even have ridden in them on occasion.

The first airships were of Nomad origin, nearly seven hundred years ago. They devised a way to trap heat from fires beneath sheets of fabric attached to wooden, raft-like vessels. Their invention eased the weight of these vessels, allowing their horses to pull normally impossible loads across the plains.

As their land changed and became the Lobhi desert, they adapted the vessels to drift over the sands. Nomads have a very airship-centric society. Pilots and other airship workers are highly respected. They improved the technology, adding steam engines and lighter-than-air gasses. The versions in use today are not pulled by any draft animal and can also be built bigger and heavier.

The various airships used during our modern era are classified by their size and capacity:

- **Glider:** Only some will classify gliders as airships, usually depending on if the glider has been outfitted with some manner of propulsion or a balloon to provide lift. Gliders may also refer to an airship of Djimbuka origin, as this technology was perfected there. Gliders typically have rigid frames with stiff fabric stretched and affixed as a sort of membrane. The largest gliders can carry up to four people, including the pilot.

- **Skimmer:** Skimmers are small, single-person vessels of Teraltian design. Many of these are not powered and rely only on air currents. That type launches typically from the cargo hold of a larger airship. Steam-powered skimmers can be outfitted with small guns, but are not impressive fighters.

- **Cloudskipper:** These are small ships with a short range. They are a favorite of the Imperial forces, as they are large and nimble enough to make formidable gunships, with crews of 2-4.

- **Zeppelin:** There is much variety within the classification of zeppelin. These airships can have both an engine and balloons, no engine, or no balloons. Any balloons of lighter-than-air gasses vary in shape and number, though most that I have seen are lifted by a single, massive balloon. They most famously are used as ferries for cargo and passengers between the land and the floating cities. Depending on the size, they might have a handful of crewmembers or all the way up to fifteen diligent people keeping the airship aloft and on track! Larger ones may have skimmers or cloudskippers among their cargo.

- **Rukh:** Massive and imposing, rukhs are kept aloft by burning the same gas as floating cities. Their engines are identical as well, if scaled down. They are prohibitively expensive to maintain, and as such are only really used by military forces and pirates. They are a home base for upwards of fifty crew and can carry large amounts of cargo as well as many smaller airships.

Acknowledgements

This collection comprises so much of went behind on the scenes while making the Automazombs books. These are the stories and backstories that we made because we loved exploring aspects of this shared world. If you've enjoyed this book, with all of its odds and ends of lore, then this acknowledgement is for you, dear reader. You are our kind of people.

About the Authors

Dex Greenbright is an illustrator as well as a sci-fi & fantasy author. He makes his home in Chicago and can usually be found writing in a cozy little corner of his local coffeeshop. For more of his writing and art, please visit dexgreenbright.com.

Victoria Bitters has been a scribbler of macabre tales since she was a kid. She is a Chicagoland librarian and practices other deadly arts, too.

Jessica L. Lim is a wandering teacher who has taught in Japan, England, and across the Chicagoland area. She would love to bring back Firefly and is the proud owner of a budgerigar named Max.

CPSIA information can be obtained
at www.ICGtesting.com
Printed in the USA
BVHW081031080822
644064BV00005B/173

9 781088 036822